Also by Lisa Graff

Far Away
The Great Treehouse War
A Clatter of Jars
Lost in the Sun
Absolutely Almost
A Tangle of Knots
Double Dog Dare
Sophie Simon Solves Them All
Umbrella Summer
The Life and Crimes of Bernetta Wallflower
The Thing About Georgie

LISA GRAFF

PHILOMEL

PHILOMEL

An imprint of Penguin Random House LLC, New York

First published in the United States of America by Philomel,
an imprint of Penguin Random House LLC, 2023

Copyright © 2023 by Lisa Graff

Penguin supports copyright. Copyright fuels creativity, encourages diverse voices,
promotes free speech, and creates a vibrant culture. Thank you for buying an authorized
edition of this book and for complying with copyright laws by not reproducing, scanning, or
distributing any part of it in any form without permission. You are supporting writers and
allowing Penguin to continue to publish books for every reader.

Philomel is a registered trademark of Penguin Random House LLC.
The Penguin colophon is a registered trademark of Penguin Books Limited.

Visit us online at PenguinRandomHouse.com.

Library of Congress Cataloging-in-Publication Data is available.

ISBN 9781524738624

1st Printing

Printed in the United States of America

LSCH

Edited by Jill Santopolo
Design by Opal Roengchai
Text set in Hoefler Text

This book is a work of fiction. Any references to historical events, real people,
or real places are used fictitiously. Other names, characters, places, and events are
products of the author's imagination, and any resemblance to actual events
or places or persons, living or dead, is entirely coincidental.

The publisher does not have any control over and does not assume
any responsibility for author or third-party websites or their content.

To all the amazing grandmothers and nurturers who've
lifted me up throughout my life, most especially:

Grandma Loaive

Grandma Rita

Auntie Dana

Uncle Roger

Daisy

Frances

and

Grandmom Lena

A Playlist for 1993

Intro "Another Night" / Real McCoy

1. "All I Wanna Do" / Sheryl Crow
2. "I'll Do It Anyway" / The Lemonheads
3. "I'll Be There" / Eternal
4. "Found Out About You" / Gin Blossoms
5. "The River of Dreams" / Billy Joel
6. "Anytime You Need a Friend" / Mariah Carey
7. "Break It Down Again" / Tears for Fears
8. "Whoops Now" / Janet Jackson
9. "All You Have to Do" / Boy Krazy
10. "Human Behaviour" / Björk
11. "What Is Love" / Haddaway
12. "Come to My Window" / Melissa Etheridge
13. "Someday I Suppose" / The Mighty Mighty Bosstones
14. "Mmm Mmm Mmm Mmm" / Crash Test Dummies
15. "What's Up?" / 4 Non Blondes
16. "Mr. Jones" / Counting Crows
17. "Linger" / The Cranberries
18. "Ice Cream" / Sarah McLachlan
19. "Explain It to Me" / Liz Phair
20. "No Rain" / Blind Melon
21. "Rock Bottom" / Babyface
22. "Revolution 1993" / Jamiroquai
23. "Mending Fences" / Restless Heart
24. "Burning Bridges" / Collective Soul
25. "Everybody Hurts" / R.E.M.

26. "Already There" / The Goo Goo Dolls

27. "Jurassic Park" / "Weird Al" Yankovic

28. "Come Undone" / Duran Duran

29. "The Key, the Secret" / Urban Cookie Collective

30. "Run to You" / Whitney Houston

31. "I Keep Coming Back" / The Afghan Whigs

32. "It's Alright" / Jeremy Jordan

33. "Changes [Remix]" / Shai

34. "Back Together Again" / Sybil

35. "You Mean the World to Me" / Toni Braxton

Outro "Now & Forever" / Carole King

Another Night

In most ways, Gap Bend, Pennsylvania, was just like any other small town. It had grocery stores and parks and an ice cream parlor and a pet shop. Kids were born, kids went to school, kids grew up. Some of those kids, when they became adults, moved off to other places. Many stayed and had kids of their own, and those kids went to school and grew up, and some of them moved, and some of them stayed. Throughout the years, some things about the town—the number of stoplights, the size of the public pool—changed, and other things—the names of the streets, the location of Town Hall—stayed the same.

But there was at least one thing about Gap Bend that wasn't like anywhere else.

Every second Saturday in June, the Gap Bend Preservation Society transformed the local public school into a wonderland of festivities in order to celebrate a specific year from history. Three years ago, at the 1975 Time Hop, everyone snarfed down Pop Rocks and Peppermint Patties while watching *Jaws* and playing *Wheel of Fortune* with actual cash prizes. When they celebrated 1886 last year, the Junior History Club put on an elaborate reenactment of President Cleveland's White House wedding, and afterward everyone headed outside to sip Coca-Cola and snack on California oranges while making the trek up the half-sized re-creation of the Statue of Liberty. The Time Hop was a day-long blowout, with everything from a one-act play written and acted by a student volunteer committee to an "Epic Epoch" fashion show, open to anyone who wanted to participate. For just one day at the end of spring, Gap Bend, Pennsylvania, was, without a doubt, the most magical place on the planet.

So when she received the flyer in the mail, twelve-year-old McKinley O'Dair was mostly concerned with the fabulous costume she might create. This would be her first time sewing her very own outfit for the fashion show, so she was delighted to learn that this year's theme was 1993—a true fashion lover's gold mine. Oversize flannel shirts, teeny-tiny crop tops, and lots and lots of denim. It also happened to be the year that McKinley's dad was in sixth grade—the same grade that she attended now, in 2018. But at the time, that didn't seem to McKinley like anything more than an uncanny coincidence.

What McKinley didn't know—what almost no one knew, except for those who'd had to learn the hard way—was that much more happened on the day of the Time Hop than a simple party. There was something else that happened, too. Something much bigger. Something almost unbelievable. McKinley wouldn't've believed it if someone had told her about it beforehand.

But that was the thing, of course. No one told her. Those who didn't know couldn't. And those who did chose not to.

And so twelve-year-old McKinley O'Dair headed into that June day with absolutely no idea about the ways in which her world was about to change forever.

1

All I Wanna Do

Later, what would strike McKinley O'Dair most about that Friday afternoon was just how completely normal it was. Her best friend, Meg, was propped upside down on the living room couch, her brown hair brushing the floor and her feet halfway up the wall, studying for the FACTS regional championship. Aunt Connie was pacing across the carpet on her phone, cheering on a new client. And McKinley was seated next to Grandma Bev in the corner of the room, both of them humming away at their side-by-side sewing machines as they put the finishing touches on their costumes for tomorrow's Time Hop.

McKinley had never felt nearly so proud of anything she'd ever sewn as she was of that outfit. The idea had been hers, the design had been hers, and the make had been hers. She was wearing nearly all of it already—a shiny silver spaghetti strap dress over a white baby doll tee, a lace choker necklace, butterfly clips in her red-brown hair, and clunky Doc Martens boots. And although *technically* she was smack in the middle of living through 2018, McKinley wouldn't have been at all out of place in the year 1993. As soon as she finished up the last seam on the denim vest, she'd be ready to walk across the stage in the fashion show tomorrow and let everyone see how hard she'd worked.

"Okay," McKinley said at last, tugging the vest out from under the needle. She trimmed the threads and held it up. "What do you think?"

"It's amazing!" Meg declared, flipping herself upright for a better look. "You're super talented, McKinley, seriously."

But Grandma Bev, who wasn't always as quick to offer praise, was carefully inspecting the garment. "Sea—seam," she said, running the fingers of her good hand over the vest's raw edges.

"I know," McKinley replied. Normally she'd never have left any piece unfinished—Grandma Bev had taught her better than that. "But the denim's so thick. I couldn't fold it over to . . ." She trailed off when Grandma Bev held up one finger. McKinley knew what that meant: there was a better way. "Ooh, show me."

McKinley scooched her folding chair closer to watch as Grandma Bev dug through her box of fabric remnants, selecting a nice soft piece of seersucker, then got to work cutting it, inch by inch. Between every cut, Grandma Bev set down her scissors, shifted the book that she'd placed on top of the fabric to weigh it down, and took back up the scissors to cut again. Since she'd had her stroke, long before McKinley was born, Grandma Bev had to do everything with her left hand, and she was not left handed. But that hadn't kept her from the things she loved— she'd just found new ways to make them happen.

It wasn't until Grandma Bev began to attach the strip of seersucker along the inner vest seams that McKinley realized what she must be up to. "Oh, I saw this on YouTube!" McKinley said, bouncing a little in her seat. "It's a Hong Kong seam, right? You fold the seersucker over next? To cover the rough edge?" Grandma Bev nodded, starting up her machine. "Cool." When she'd finished demonstrating, Grandma Bev handed over the vest so McKinley could try for herself.

Once McKinley had gotten into a good rhythm on the machine, she got back to her other job, too—helping Meg study.

"All right, here's a good one," McKinley told Meg, pausing her sewing so she could enlarge the sample question on her phone. "Name the layers of the earth's atmosphere."

Meg repositioned herself upside down on the couch. (She said the extra blood flow to her brain helped her concentrate.) "Layer one," she began, pointing and flexing her toes against the wall. *Point, flex, point, flex.* "Troposphere. Two: stratosphere." She glanced at McKinley. "Three . . . metasphere?"

"*Meso*sphere," McKinley corrected, squinting at the tough words to make sure she read them right. At the machine beside her, Grandma Bev lifted her foot off her pedal so Meg could hear more clearly. "Then it's thermosphere, then exosphere, and ionosphere."

Meg threw her hands over her face. "Gah!" she shouted. "I *knew* that! I'm just getting so nervous thinking about being up there all by myself for the first time ever and—"

"You are going to rock this," McKinley assured her. "I was just weighing you down before."

The truth was, the Federation of American Competitive Trivia for Students had always been more Meg's thing than McKinley's. Sure, it had been a blast going to competitions together over the years, silently cheering for each other between rounds onstage. Even all the studying had been pretty fun because they were doing it together. But McKinley was ready to find something new to do together, or, as Aunt Connie would say, to "shake up their routine." McKinley already had her eye on all sorts of activities they could try out—babysitting, joining the school's Film Appreciation Club, volunteering at the Gap Bend Animal Shelter . . .

Unfortunately, Meg didn't seem quite as ready to move on as McKinley was. She'd needed a little push. So McKinley had made Meg a promise: If they got to nationals in DC, they'd stick with FACTS another year. If not, Meg had agreed to give something else a whirl. Which *might* have been the reason McKinley had had a hard time looking sad after she'd gotten kicked out during round two of the Pennsylvania state meet last month.

"Come on," McKinley told Meg kindly. If this was Meg's last year in FACTS, McKinley wanted to make sure she went out with a bang. "Hit me with a memory story."

Meg stared at her toes, thinking. *Point, flex, point, flex.* It was McKinley's dad who'd introduced Meg to the concept of "memory stories"—little tales that strung weird facts together and made them easier to remember. It was just one of the tricks Meg used to help herself with her learning disability. As McKinley's dad liked to say, "A struggle is simply an opportunity to find a creative solution."

"Got it!" Meg said finally. "I won a—*troposphere*—trophy, because of my—*stratosphere*—strategy for not—*mesosphere*—messing up my—*thermosphere*—thermal underwear when I—*exosphere*—exercise. And now I've got my—*ionosphere*—"

And because they'd been friends since before either of them could *say* "friends," McKinley knew exactly where Meg's brain was headed.

"*Eye-on-a-sphere!*" McKinley hollered.

Only, of course, Meg said it at the same exact time.

"*Pretzel point!*" McKinley cried—at exactly the same time as Meg again. "*Pretzel point! Pretzel point!*" It ended up taking eight tries before Meg finally beat her.

"Muh—Muh—Meg wuh—won," Grandma Bev declared, with her familiar half smile.

"Shoot!" McKinley shouted, but she was laughing. At the end of the week, whoever had the fewest points had to buy the other friend a soft pretzel during lunch. (Since they always split the pretzel anyway, losing was almost as good as winning.)

For the next half an hour, McKinley sewed and quizzed. Meg flexed and memorized. Grandma Bev pinned and snipped. And Aunt Connie paced and gabbed. Until, at last, McKinley finished the final seam on her vest. She slipped her arms through the armholes and turned a circle to show it off. "Better?" she asked, smoothing her palms over the skirt of her shiny silver dress.

"It's puh—perfect," Grandma Bev breathed. Her eyes were shiny, and she was smiling that familiar half smile. "Yuh—*You're* perfect."

McKinley beamed.

Aunt Connie finally ended her phone call. "You look delightful, kid," she told McKinley. "You know what would really top off the ensemble, though?" And, seemingly from nowhere, she pulled out a crab-shaped hat and plopped it on McKinley's head. It was red and fuzzy, with two big red claws and giant floppy eyes sprouting from the top. On the back were embroidered the words CONNIE'S C.R.A.B.S.!

"Oh, yes," McKinley said with a laugh. "*Very* chic, thank you."

"Of course," Aunt Connie replied. "You know I've got plenty more where that came from."

She wasn't kidding.

When Aunt Connie had started her life coaching business a few years back, she'd leaned hard into the crab theme—crab hats, crab flash drives, crab stress balls. Any promotional item that *could* be shaped like a crab *was* shaped like a crab. And it seemed to be working for her. Because even though McKinley's dad liked to refer to life coaching as "bossing people around for money," Aunt Connie had hundreds of loyal clients who swore by her methods. With only five simple steps, Aunt Connie claimed, anyone could change into the best version of themselves. All you had to do was "get crabby":

1. COUNT your blessings.
2. RIGHT your wrongs.
3. ASSESS your neighbors.
4. BETTER your world.
5. SHAKE up your routine.

Technically, Aunt Connie wasn't anyone's aunt, but she'd more than earned the title. She and Grandma Bev had been friends since *they'd* gone to Gap Bend Public School together. After Grandma Bev's husband had died when McKinley's dad was only a baby, Aunt Connie had flown in from the West Coast to help out—and somehow never thought to book a return ticket. Years later, when a stroke took away most of Grandma Bev's words and half her smile, it was Aunt Connie who made sure McKinley's dad finished up school and "didn't become a total no-goodnik." McKinley liked to think that this was the kind of friendship she and Meg would have when they were older (only hopefully with fewer terry cloth tracksuits, because no matter what Aunt Connie said, those things were *not* flattering).

Aunt Connie's phone rang again. "*Sorry!*" she mouthed to the rest of them. "*Client!*" And she took off out the door, waving at McKinley's father, who was just climbing the front steps on his way home from work.

McKinley's eyes went wide when she spotted her dad. In all the excitement of finishing her Time Hop costume and helping Meg study, she'd completely forgotten to start prepping dinner. Which may not have been such a huge deal to most parents, but McKinley's dad did not take his dinner schedule lightly.

Later, McKinley would wonder if it had been the meat loaf's fault. If she'd just remembered to start dinner, maybe none of what happened next would've happened at all. Or maybe it was all that time she'd spent helping Meg. Or the extra attention she'd paid to her Time Hop costume. Maybe, just maybe, it was the little white lie she'd been telling for the past month. But whatever it was that set things into motion, the series of events that would begin to unravel in just a few short hours would change McKinley's life forever.

They'd change everything, really.

2

I'll Do It Anyway

There was a chalkboard sign in McKinley's kitchen that read DINNER THIS WEEK! and, below that, seven spaces in which to write each night's meal. McKinley had joked once that, seeing as how their weekly dinner rotation had stayed exactly the same for the entire twelve years she'd been alive, the sign really ought to say DINNER THIS CENTURY!

Her dad had not found that especially amusing.

So when McKinley realized that she'd forgotten to start dinner that Friday evening, she decided her only option was to stall for time. At least that way Meg could flee to safety before her father blew a fuse.

"Hey, Dad!" she greeted her father as he came through the door. She darted her eyes at Meg like, *Run! Run for your life!* "How was work?"

"Awful," her father said, shrugging out of his boring gray suit jacket. "Look, McKinley, there's something I need to talk to you about."

"Sure, sure," she replied. She darted her eyes again at Meg. But Meg must've been super nervous about the competition tomorrow night, because she was way off her eye-reading game. She didn't even budge from her spot on the couch. "There's something, uh, I wanted to talk to you about, too. Uh . . ." She thought quickly. "They're showing *Jurassic Park* at the Cineplex next weekend." That's what she landed on. "Because of the Time Hop, I guess, and because it's, like, the twenty-fifth anniversary. Wanna go?"

In reply, McKinley's dad rubbed at his crooked nose. He'd broken it the very same day that Grandma Bev had had her stroke—a constant reminder of one of the worst days of his life. "I don't think so," he told her. "You know I'm not much for movies."

"It's supposed to be really good," she said, even though she knew he'd never go. She wasn't sure her father had *ever* been to a movie theater. (Seriously, who didn't like movies?) McKinley and Meg went whenever they could. They especially loved talking about their favorite cheesy bad films with Miguel Rosas, who owned the theater in town.

Her dad let out a long *mmm*, which was the noise he made when he thought he knew better than you. It was a noise that drove McKinley up the wall.

And then he sniffed the air.

"Why can't I smell the meat loaf?" he asked. Over on the couch, Meg silently slapped a hand over her mouth, finally catching on. McKinley's stomach lurched as he headed closer to the kitchen. "It's just my luck the oven breaks *now*," he went on, "what with the day I'm having. No one's going to be able to come look at it till Monday, so what am I supposed to do with the chicken for tomorrow? Not to mention the—"

"Dad!" McKinley hadn't meant to shout, really. It was just that when her dad started doom spiraling, it was best to cut him off as soon as possible. "The oven's not broken. I forgot to start dinner."

"What?" he asked, turning. He looked confused, like McKinley had said she wanted to knit sweaters for boa constrictors. "But you always start dinner before I get home. It's a whole system."

"I'm really sorry," McKinley told him. If her dad ever decided to write the world's most boring autobiography, he would absolutely title the thing *It's a Whole System!* "I was working on my Time Hop costume and helping Meg study and . . . Maybe we could order a pizza or something."

Apparently, that comment made the boa constrictor sweater thing seem absolutely reasonable.

"Do you know why we have a schedule?" McKinley's father asked, pinching the bridge of his crooked nose. "Because I am a single father with a twelve-year-old daughter and a sixty-five-year-old mother to take care of and only so much time in the week to do it. So having a dinner schedule makes it easier to shop."

"I know that," McKinley began, "but would it really hurt if just this once—"

"If we were to order pizza tonight," her father told her, "that would mean that the turkey I bought for the meat loaf would go to waste."

"Couldn't you just have meat loaf tomorrow?" Meg wondered.

But when McKinley's dad turned to answer, she froze, like maybe he wouldn't realize it was her who'd said it.

"Tomorrow is chicken," he said. And he wasn't trying to be mean about it, McKinley could tell. But he didn't give the idea even a nanosecond of thought, either. "It's a whole—"

"A whole system," McKinley finished for him. "Yeah."

At that, her dad seemed to soften. "Look, I know it was an honest mistake. Sometimes I worry I put too much responsibility on you." He let out a hefty sigh. "Come on, we'll start the meat loaf together, okay?"

Meg insisted on helping, too, since she said she felt partially responsible for distracting McKinley. And things were actually going quite well for a while there, with McKinley on potato duty and Meg trimming the green beans. McKinley's dad was even doing all the gucky turkey-mushing, so McKinley didn't have to. And then McKinley made the mistake of asking her father, "So what was it you wanted to talk about?"

He squirted some more ketchup into the bowl of ground turkey. "I'm going to have to work tomorrow," he told her. He sighed. "Dan Kotsberg missed his deadline on our big account, which made everything snowball and . . . Anyway, it means I'm going to miss the whole Time Hop. And I'm going to need you to watch your grandmother. All day. You'll need to give her her meds at lunch."

McKinley set down her peeler. "Ugh, I'm sorry, Dad, that stinks. I can watch Grandma Bev, though, no problem."

"Thanks, McKinley," her father said. He seemed genuinely relieved. "You're being really mature about this, and I appreciate it. I know you worked really hard on your costume, so I'm sorry you'll have to miss the fashion show."

Beside her at the stove, McKinley felt Meg's body go stiff.

"What do you mean?" McKinley asked. "Why would I have to miss the fashion show?"

Her father frowned. "It's a lot of medication, McKinley," he replied—like McKinley didn't know that. She'd given Grandma Bev her meds before (okay, not a lot of times, but *some*times). "And she has to take it with food, at noon. So you may leave for the Time Hop after lunch. But since the fashion show is before that, I'm afraid you'll have to miss it."

"They have food there," McKinley argued.

"Of course they do. But if she takes it here, I can set everything out the way I always do. We have a whole system."

"I'm sure it wouldn't be that—"

"McKinley." Her father cut her off. "If you couldn't remember to start a meat loaf tonight, I'm not about to entrust you with an entire pharmacy."

McKinley did her best to stay calm. This was not happening. It *couldn't* happen. "Well, maybe Aunt Connie can stay with her, then," she suggested. "Just until after lunch." McKinley would be gutted not to have Grandma Bev at the fashion show to cheer her on, but it was better than not being there at all.

"She's DJ'ing the Time Hop, remember?" It was Meg who said it, and as soon as McKinley turned her way, she looked like she would've rather jumped into the boiling green bean water. "*Sorry*," she whispered.

But it wasn't Meg who McKinley was mad at. "This isn't fair,"

15

she told her dad. The silver fabric of McKinley's perfect spaghetti strap dress was suddenly clinging to her legs. Her arms couldn't move inside her vest. Her choker was . . . *choking* her. "I worked so hard."

"I'm sorry, kiddo," her dad said. And maybe he did look a little bit sorry. But it wasn't enough. "That's just the way things are. If one person falls down on the job, everyone else has to scramble. That's why we stick to the system, right?"

McKinley knew there was no arguing. Not when it came to her dad and his system. And so she replied, "Right." Just the way he wanted.

Even if she knew it wasn't.

"I'm really sorry you can't be in the fashion show," Meg said as McKinley walked her down the front steps. She looked as gutted by it all as McKinley felt. "I won't clap for a single person, just because they're not you."

That was the first thing that had made McKinley crack a smile in twenty minutes. "If there was still a way I could go, without my dad knowing," she said slowly, kicking at the chip in the porch railing as she thought, "would you help me?"

Meg blinked at her. "What do you mean?"

"I can totally give Grandma Bev her medicine while we're there," McKinley told her. "That's not a big deal. But I do need someone to keep an eye on her during the fashion show."

Meg didn't even need a second to think it over. "I'll do it," she said.

"Oh my gosh, Meg, you are the *best*. I'll text you when my dad leaves in the morning, okay?"

"You got it." Meg started down the steps. And then she turned, right at the last step, to shout, "*Olive loaf!*" Same as she always did. Their secret friend code.

"*Olive loaf!*" McKinley hollered back. Same as always. Then she went back inside for dinner, without any idea of what was about to happen.

Or any idea of *when*.

3

I'll Be There

In the twelve years she'd been alive, McKinley O'Dair had never missed a single Time Hop. But the second she stepped through the doors of Gap Bend Public School that Saturday morning, she could already tell that this year's was going to be better than all those other Time Hops combined.

"Wuh—whoa," Grandma Bev breathed, pushing back the rim of her blossomed hat as she craned her neck upward. Towering above them in the school's entryway were two colossal dinosaur skeletons. One was a T. rex and one—a brontosaurus, probably—had a neck so long a car could drive down it. Their bones were the color of mud, and their teeth were knives. A banner, black with red-and-yellow letters, was suspended from the ceiling above.

WHEN 1993 RULED THE TIME HOP

"It's just like in *Jurassic Park*," said a familiar voice. McKinley turned to see Meg's parents, Jackie and Ron, entering behind them. "The movie came out that year," Jackie went on. She was wearing an ugly two-piece white nylon tracksuit with purple, green, and red stripes, made even awfuller somehow by the addition of white socks and white Keds shoes. "The first one, I mean. And it was *huge*."

Beside her, Ron snorted. "Ha, *huge*," he said. He was wearing a mustard-yellow shirt buttoned all the way up to the chin.

"Good one, hon." Without even looking, Jackie and Ron managed a perfect high five.

McKinley loved what a goofy team Meg's parents were. Her own parents had gotten divorced when she was two, and now McKinley's mom lived all the way in Virginia.

McKinley checked her phone. Plenty of time until the fashion show started, and yet . . .

Jackie must've sensed what McKinley was thinking. "Meg'll be here in a few minutes," she assured her. "She wanted to make sure she had everything together for FACTS."

McKinley let her shoulders relax a little. She'd spent ages that morning snapping pics of all Grandma Bev's medications and her dad's instructions about them to be sure she got everything right. (Grandma Bev, of course, had been totally chill about sneaking out. She wanted to be at the fashion show just as badly as McKinley did.) Still, McKinley would feel better once Meg was here.

"We're driving you to the competition tonight, right?" Ron asked. "We're leaving at four sharp. Getting into Philly on a Saturday night . . . I wouldn't be surprised if this event was organized by tow truck drivers."

"Can't wait," McKinley told him.

McKinley was taking a photo of the dinosaurs when her

phone lit up. Her dad. Probably calling to give her another lecture about His Whole System. McKinley clicked ignore and stuffed the phone into the pocket on the back of Grandma Bev's wheelchair. She could get just as great a lecture over voicemail.

As they passed underneath the dinosaur skeletons and entered the GBPS gymnasium, McKinley had to blink to take it all in. Every square inch of her regular old run-of-the-mill, get-whacked-in-the-forehead-by-a-dodgeball-inside-it school gym had been transformed.

"Ooh, *Dawn and the Surfer Ghost!*" Jackie shrieked as they passed the book station.

"Uh-oh, now we've lost her," Ron muttered as his wife skittered over. Jackie was the editor of a literary magazine and always had her nose buried inside some book or seven. "I'll have to pry her away before we leave so I can kick her butt at *Street Fighter II*. That was our first date, you know," he informed McKinley and Grandma Bev. "A *Street Fighter II* competition at Galaxy Arcade. Jackie likes to claim she won, but I'm pretty sure it was me."

McKinley's gaze was pulled toward the dozens of old-school television sets—boxy, with antennae and everything—stacked one on top of the other against the wall beside them. Each TV was sitting on top of what Ron explained was a VCR, and there were shelves and shelves stuffed full of video tapes inside plastic Blockbuster cases for guests to browse through and watch. McKinley tilted her head back for a better look at the large neon red sign just to the right of the door.

BE KIND, REWIND!

And she was still standing there, minding her own business, when she was bumped into by somebody hurrying past.

"O'Dair," the person grumbled at her when he saw who he'd knocked into. It was Mr. Jones, McKinley's sixth-grade homeroom and history teacher. "Of course. Always causing trouble."

"Uh, sorry," McKinley said. She knew better than to argue. Mr. Jones had had it in for her since the first day of kindergarten, when she tripped over a fifth grader who was planking in the hallway and Mr. Jones blamed *her* for creating a roadblock. Today he seemed especially tense. His whole body (white, thin, and stringy) seemed to be scowling. Even his *hair* (white, thin, and stringy) was scowling somehow.

Mr. Jones scrunched his face at McKinley like a balled-up sock. "I'm keeping a special eye on you today, O'Dair," he told her before stomping off across the gym.

Grandma Bev turned around to look at McKinley with *What the heck?* eyebrows.

"I wouldn't take it personally," Ron told them. "Rufus Jones has been that way since *I* had him."

Next they checked out the refreshments. The candy selection was on point—Warheads, BarNones, Choc 'N' Orange Twix, Dweebs—and the savory options looked promising, too. There was Goodfella's frozen pizza and re-creations of a McDonald's sandwich called the "McLobster." McKinley sampled a bowl of Sprinkle Spangles cereal while Jackie danced (badly) and sang along (loudly) to a tune DJ Connie was blasting, which was about something called a "Shoop." But McKinley hadn't even gotten in three spoonfuls before her phone rang again.

Her dad.

And there was a voicemail and three new texts.

McKinley clicked the phone dark.

They explored for a while longer. McKinley's dad kept calling. Meg kept texting to say she was almost there.

"Hey, Jackie and Ron," McKinley finally asked. It was starting to get late. "Could you help Grandma Bev find a seat for the show? Meg said she'd sit with her, but she's not here yet, and I need to sign in."

"Of course," Jackie replied. "Not a problem."

"Thanks." McKinley handed her phone to Grandma Bev to take photos, then headed to the sign-in table beside the gym stage. There were tons of amazing costumes this year, McKinley noted as she joined the back of the line—Philly Eagles Zubaz pants and baby doll crop tees and big bright, ugly sweaters and flannel. So. Much. Flannel. McKinley smoothed the silver fabric of her dress against her legs. This was heaven. It didn't matter that her dad was being unreasonable or that she'd had to sneak out just to be there. Because the moment the announcer declared, *"And next, a costume created by McKinley O'Dair!"* it would all be worth it.

There was a tap on her shoulder.

"You came!" McKinley cried when she set eyes on Meg. "And you look awesome!"

"My mom found it in the back of her closet," Meg said. She spun to give McKinley a better view of the blue-and-black-checked bodysuit and high-waisted shorts. "Isn't it great?"

McKinley grinned. "Maybe next year you can be in the fashion show, too. Grandma Bev and I will help you with your costume." She jumped an excited little jump. "I can even teach you to sew if you want. We'll have so much more free time now that we're not doing FACTS anymore."

That made Meg scrunch her eyebrows together. "What do you mean we're not doing FACTS anymore?"

McKinley frowned. It wasn't like Meg to go back on a promise. Was it possible she'd forgotten? "We said that if we didn't make it to the finals in DC, then we'd quit for good," McKinley reminded her.

"Right," Meg said slowly. Her eyebrows were still scrunched. "But I might still make it. We won't know for sure till tonight."

McKinley felt like a lemon being squeezed. "The deal was if one of us loses, we quit," she said. "And I lost at state last month."

"The deal was if we *both* lose," Meg replied. And then, slowly, she narrowed her eyes, like something had just occurred to her. "Did you get that question wrong on purpose?"

McKinley took a little too long to respond.

And for Meg, that was response enough.

"I *knew* it!" Meg shouted. McKinley could sense the people around them pretending not to pay attention. "Everyone knows the capital of Paraguay!"

"Not everyone," McKinley muttered.

Meg stared at her. Straight in the eyes. "But *you* do," she said.

McKinley didn't argue.

"I can't believe this!" Meg threw her hands in the air. "How could you do that? Why would you lie?"

McKinley stayed calm. She and Meg weren't fighting, she knew, because they had never fought before. They were just having a little misunderstanding. "I knew if I didn't," she explained, "you'd stay in FACTS forever. Keep doing the same old things as always."

"So?" Meg asked. Her eyes were growing larger and larger now. If McKinley didn't patch things up soon, her friend wouldn't have room on her face for her nose.

"*So*," McKinley said, "I was trying to look out for you. It was time to shake up your routine, like Aunt Connie always says."

Apparently, those were not the words that would make Meg's eyes get smaller.

"It sounds like you were looking out for *you*," Meg replied. "And if you were so sick of FACTS, you could've just said so."

"No," McKinley said. How had this gone so sideways, when all she'd wanted was to help her best friend? "It's just that I know you get nervous about trying new things. I don't know if it's because of your learning disability or you just get scared or what. But sometimes I feel like, if I don't push you, you won't do *anything*. I was trying to be a good friend."

Meg crossed her arms over her chest. "A good friend wouldn't try to change me into somebody else," she said. And her voice had a twinge of meanness to it that McKinley had never heard before.

McKinley only realized her mouth was hanging open when she spied her reflection in the Oakley sunglasses of the guy next to her. The man quickly looked away, like he hadn't been watching McKinley's friendship implode in the middle of the Time Hop.

"Oh yeah?" McKinley huffed. Suddenly she wanted to make Meg feel just as lemon-squeezy bad as she did. "Well, a good friend wouldn't get mad at someone who was just looking out for them."

This was where Meg would apologize, McKinley figured. This was where she'd realize what she'd said, and how mean it had sounded, and where she'd tell McKinley how much she really did need her.

Only, she didn't.

"I guess I'm not a good friend, then," Meg snapped.

McKinley's heart snapped, too.

"I guess you're not," McKinley said back.

There was a moment—the tiniest sliver of a second—where McKinley knew that she could probably fix it. All she had to do, as Meg moved to storm away, was to call out to her. "*Olive loaf!*" she'd holler. Same as they always did. Their special code. And they'd still be mad at each other, sure, but she and Meg would still be her and Meg. And they'd figure it all out.

"McKinley? Honey?" It was Miss Carlisle at the sign-in table. "If you still want to be in the fashion show, I really need you to sign in."

McKinley watched as Meg walked farther and farther across the gym floor. Still within shouting distance, just barely.

"Okay," McKinley said. And she turned her back on Meg, and she picked up a pen.

4

Found Out About You

The first official event of the Time Hop, every year, was a one-act play. It was always entirely created by students from Gap Bend Public School—costumes, props, all of it—and it was always a blast. McKinley enjoyed getting a close-up view of things, watching from backstage as she waited for the fashion show to begin. This year, the play included a rap. It was ridiculously goofy.

> Bill Clinton starts as 42.
> X-Files *asks us what is true.*
> NASA *loses touch with Mars.*
> The Mickey Mouse Club *launches stars.*
> *A Great Blizzard slams us all with snow.*
> *Barbie speaks for G.I. Joe.*
> *Beanie Babies hit store racks.*
> *We meet the Animaniacs.*
> *And one question that we won't tire of*
> *Is: What won't Meat Loaf do for love?*

Normally McKinley would've gotten a huge kick out of something so silly (even if she didn't understand every reference). But just at the moment, she had butterflies in her stomach that were flipping nauseous somersaults. She wasn't entirely sure if it was because she was about to show off an outfit of her own creation for the very first time or because she'd just had her only-ever fight with her best friend.

Probably a little of both.

When the play ended, McKinley joined the rest of the gym in applause. The cast filed offstage, clapping each other on the back as a song called "Whoomp! (There It Is)" came blasting through the speakers. And just like that, the fashion show had begun.

One by one, McKinley's neighbors trotted onto the stage, spinning to display their costumes. From where she was standing in the wings, McKinley could make out Grandma Bev in her wheelchair, and she looked fine. But she couldn't see much else. She wondered if Meg had stayed to cheer her on and to watch Grandma Bev, like she'd promised. She wondered if her dad had ever given up calling. (For a brief moment, McKinley even imagined she heard him hissing at her from just offstage.) But as soon as it was her turn, McKinley's worries faded away.

"*Next up,*" called the announcer, "*it's our youngest designer ever, McKinley O'Dair!*" The butterflies started up an excited rumba as McKinley stepped onto the stage. As the announcer read out the various details of her costume, McKinley twirled to show them off. And with each new piece, the crowd cheered even louder.

But maybe McKinley shouldn't have ignored all those phone calls from her father earlier.

Or the hissing offstage.

Because just as McKinley had pointed her left toe to show off her vintage Doc Martens, there came an awful *squeal*. McKinley turned to where the announcer stood and saw that somehow on the stage across from her, holding the announcer's microphone, was her father.

He began to speak.

"I'm sorry, everyone," he said into the mic. His eyes were narrowed right at McKinley. "My daughter can't finish showing you her costume, because she's not supposed to be here in the first place. McKinley, we're leaving. *Now*."

Gasps from the audience.

Confused murmurs.

Hot tears sprang to McKinley's eyes. She couldn't believe her dad. Who did something like that to their own kid? And all because she wouldn't follow his awful system for one stinking day?

Before anyone could stop her, McKinley turned on her heel, and she ran.

Down the stage steps, two at a time.

Through the crowd in their folding chairs.

On her way to the gym doors, McKinley spotted that neon sign again.

BE KIND, REWIND!

And she only had a second to think about it, but she did wonder, as she darted out the door . . . Hadn't the sign been red before?

Because now it was glowing green.

* * *

McKinley knew her father would expect her to head past the dinosaurs and out of the school. So instead, she turned a sharp right and raced down the hall, flying past classrooms without even thinking where she might be headed. She craned her neck to see if anyone was following her as she turned the corner toward the girls' bathroom.

"*Oof!*" cried Jackie as McKinley careened full force into her.

"Oh, shoot, sorry," McKinley said. Lemonade from a paper cup had sloshed all over Jackie's tracksuit top. McKinley checked once more for her dad, but there was no sign of him.

"No worries," Jackie said. "I've spilled like eight things on this jacket already. Fortunately it cleans like a dream." She pulled a wad of tissues from her purse and gave half to McKinley for her tears. "You want to talk about it?"

McKinley swiped at her eyes as she shook her head, half yes, half no. Usually McKinley could talk to Meg's mom about anything. Jackie wasn't like McKinley's dad—she was actually fun, and she cared about what McKinley had to say. But what if Meg had told her mom about their fight? What if Jackie took Meg's side? Or worse, what if Jackie found out why McKinley was running and decided to call McKinley's dad? "It's just . . ." McKinley began. A sniffle turned into a wail. "It's just . . . *everything.*"

"Oh, honey." Jackie gave McKinley another tissue. "You know, when I was your—" She stopped, listening to something down the hall. McKinley heard it, too. Footsteps, good and stompy ones. "Wait here," Jackie told her.

McKinley stood, still and tense, as Jackie turned the corner to investigate.

"If you're searching for McKinley," she heard Jackie say after a moment, "I think you should give her a little time to calm dow—"

But to McKinley's surprise, the man who responded was not her father.

"Out of my way, Yorks," Mr. Jones barked at Jackie. "That girl's not going to weasel away this time."

McKinley sucked in her breath. What crime did Mr. Jones think she'd committed now?

"You know it's Rothstein now, not Yorks," Jackie corrected him. "But fine, have it your way. After you." McKinley's stomach went tight again as she waited for Mr. Jones to turn the corner.

Only . . .

He didn't.

"What happened?" McKinley whispered to Jackie when she came back into view. "Where'd Mr. Jones go?"

Jackie twirled a set of keys that McKinley hadn't noticed her carrying before. "Let's just say he won't be bothering you for a while," she said with a sinister grin.

"You *killed* him?" McKinley shrieked.

Jackie laughed at that. "No!" she cried. "I locked him in the maintenance closet."

"You . . . what?" Suddenly McKinley thought she could make out the muffled sounds of a senior citizen pounding on a closet door. "Why?"

Jackie shrugged one shoulder. "I guess I've always wanted to. Now, let's get back to you. Tell me what's—"

That's when they heard stomping from down the hall again. And this time, McKinley was *certain* it was her father.

"Can you please lock him in a closet, too?" McKinley begged.

Jackie took a deep breath and knelt down just a little to place both hands on McKinley's shoulders. "You'll be fine," she told her. She was staring McKinley right in the eye, deadly serious. "I promise. You believe me?" McKinley nodded. "Good. And remember. If you ever need to talk, or need my help, you can come find me, anytime. Okay?"

"Okay," McKinley told her. She wiped at her eyes with the balled-up tissue. She supposed she'd have to face her father sooner or later.

"I mean it," Jackie said. The footsteps were getting closer. "Any. Time."

"Thanks," McKinley said. And despite everything, she allowed herself a tiny smile. Then, with a deep breath of courage, she took one step toward the bend in the corner to get yelled at by her dad.

But to her shock, Jackie put a hand on McKinley's chest to stop her. "No," Jackie told her. "Not yet."

And McKinley watched, confused, as Jackie reached around her to open the door of the girls' bathroom.

"*William?*" Jackie called over her shoulder. "*Is that you?*"

"*Jackie?*" It was McKinley's dad, all right, closing in on them. "*I'm looking for McKinley. Have you seen her?*"

"*Yeah!*" Jackie hollered back. "*One sec!*" And with that, she shoved McKinley inside the bathroom.

5

The River of Dreams

The bathroom door swung shut with a soft *click*, and McKinley tried to breathe deep and calm, the way they'd learned in that PE unit on meditation. Could Jackie really distract McKinley's dad long enough to stop him from going nuclear? (Well, *more* nuclear?) And would Jackie even be helping McKinley at all if she knew about her blowup with Meg?

(McKinley couldn't believe she hadn't *olive loaf*ed Meg. They'd never not *olive loaf*ed before. They were going to make up, right? *Breathe, McKinley*, she told herself. *Deep and calm.*)

McKinley caught sight of herself in the scratched-up mirror. Her face was patchy from crying, her eyes red, her auburn hair wild from running. She looked out of place inside her perfect Time Hop costume. She couldn't believe she was stuck crying in a bathroom instead of up onstage, showing off her hard work. All because of—

"Hey, Billy!"

Suddenly there was a voice from the hall. A *boy's* voice. McKinley ducked inside a stall just as the door swung open.

"Coast is clear!" the voice said, and then, laughing, two boys entered the bathroom.

McKinley peered at them through the crack in the stall door. What were they up to?

"Quick, over here!" the second boy said, bringing something to the sink. "Put those inside. No, *all* of them."

Gap Bend was a small town, so McKinley knew every kid her age by first, last, and middle name. And yet here were two boys she'd never met before. The first kid was chubby with white skin, dark curly hair, and freckles all over his legs and arms. The second boy, Billy, was skinnier and tall, also white but with reddish-brown hair. They must be someone's nephews or grandsons, McKinley figured, in town for the Time Hop. They were dressed for it, anyway—the first kid was wearing a striped polo and baggy shorts, and Billy had on a Pearl Jam T-shirt and red-and-black-checkered Vans sneakers. She squinted at them through the gap. Maybe there *was* something slightly familiar about them.

"Okay, now fill it with water and shake," Billy said. "We gotta set it off before she realizes we stole it."

McKinley pressed her eye closer to the gap. The boys appeared to be messing with some sort of homemade rocket.

"Put the cap on, quick!"

Wait a minute, a *rocket*?

With a sudden *BOOM!* and several shrieks, the rocket went *off*—straight into the bathroom ceiling, where it lodged itself tight, spewing fizzy rocket fuel in torrents all over the floor. McKinley screamed and ran out of the stall, through the stuck-rocket sprinkler, right on the heels of the two boys, who were fleeing the scene with peals of laughter. But she didn't get half-way down the short hallway before—

"Now, just you *stop right there*."

McKinley came to a screeching halt when she heard the voice, and the two boys must've sensed that an angry Mr. Jones was no one to mess with, because they halted, too. But as McKinley blinked up at her teacher, her mouth formed an *O* of surprise. She wouldn't have suspected that while he was locked in the maintenance closet, Mr. Jones would've taken the time to put on a toupee. But somehow here he was, suddenly unbald. He must've used some sort of skin cream, too, because his wrinkles looked less . . . wrinkly.

His makeover hadn't done anything to help his mood, though. Mr. Jones set his fists at his hips and narrowed his eyes. "Explain yourself, O'Dair," he growled.

McKinley gulped. But she didn't get a chance to speak.

"*Now*, Billy," Mr. Jones commanded. His eyes were focused on the boy beside her, the one in the Pearl Jam T-shirt.

McKinley felt a tingle all the way up her spine and back down again. She squinted at the kid. She squinted harder.

"*Billy O'Dair!*" Mr. Jones roared.

Some way, somehow, this boy was McKinley's . . .

"Dad?" she sputtered.

"Who are you?" the boy with the red-brown hair asked, wrinkling his nose at McKinley. He had the same gray eyes as her dad. He had the same *name* as her dad. But he was *not* her dad, obviously. Because McKinley's dad was thirty-seven. And this kid was . . . not.

The chubby kid poked Billy with his elbow. "Dude, I'm pretty sure she called you 'Dad.'"

Mr. Jones death-glared both of them. "Enough, Rothstein," he snapped. And McKinley did her second double take of the last two minutes. *Rothstein?* As in *Meg* Rothstein?

"*Ron?*" she said, eyes bugging out of her head. Was this something new they were doing for the Time Hop—bringing in kid doppelgangers of grown-up Gap Benders?

"Rothstein, get back to class," Mr. Jones snapped. "O'Dair, you're coming with me." Almost as an afterthought, he turned his attention on McKinley. "Miss, don't you have somewhere you should be?"

"How did you get out of the maintenance closet?" McKinley wondered. Something about the hallway looked weird. She couldn't put her finger on it. "Where'd Jackie go?"

Mr. Jones's only response was a throaty growl. "Wherever you're supposed to be," he told her, "you better get there, stat. Rothstein, *off*." The Ron look-alike skedaddled down the hall. "O'Dair, this way." And he marched Billy off to the principal's office, leaving McKinley alone in the strange, empty hall.

It was the lockers, she realized, spinning in a slow, incredulous circle. Her whole life, the GBPS lockers had been painted blue. Now, somehow, they were orange.

This was weird. And where had her dad and Jackie gone off to?

McKinley inched toward the gym, running her fingertips along the lockers as she went. Suddenly she wasn't feeling so well. She needed to find Grandma Bev and go home.

But when she pushed open the gym doors, McKinley stumbled back so hard she landed right on her butt.

There was no fashion show up on the gym stage.

There was no wall of TVs.

There was no refreshments table or Aunt Connie blasting music from the DJ booth or neighbors enjoying themselves in their best '90s attire.

Instead, there were kids. In gym clothes. Playing dodgeball. The squeaks of sneakers bounced off the walls.

What.

Was.

Happening.

McKinley was still sitting there, staring, when the bell rang. Within seconds, the hallway filled with kids. Lockers were slammed, backpacks were zipped, crumpled papers were tossed in high arcs across the hall. McKinley scrambled to her feet as the crowd pushed its way toward the front door.

The front door.

"You okay?" a kid asked her. It was a girl with two french braids in her hair and braces with alternating neon-pink and yellow bands.

"Where are the dinosaurs?" McKinley asked. The two enormous *Jurassic Park* dinosaur skeletons were gone. The banner, too.

"Dinosaurs?" the girl asked.

"They were just there," McKinley said. "For the Time Hop."

The girl raised an eyebrow at McKinley. "I have no idea what dinosaurs you're talking about," she said slowly, "and the Time Hop's not till next week." She peered a little closer at McKinley. "Do you need the nurse or something?"

McKinley shook her head. "I'm fine," she said. (Although . . . was she?) "I just . . . need to find my grandma. She needs to take her meds soon, and she's probably worried about me." McKinley patted the sides of her vest, suddenly furious at herself for not taking the time to sew in pockets. "Can I borrow your phone for a sec?"

For whatever reason, that made the girl's second eyebrow go up. "Sorry," she said, "but I don't let weird strangers into my house." And with that, she turned and walked outside with everyone else.

McKinley had heard, once, that the only real way to know if you were in a dream was to read something—a book or a computer screen or whatever—and then turn around and look at it again. Because apparently, in dreams, you can't read something the exact same way twice. So—*deep breath in, deep breath out*—McKinley scanned the area until she spotted a bulletin board near the main office. By the time she'd made her way over, the hallway was almost completely empty.

THERE'S STILL TIME TO JOIN THE TIME HOP STUDENT VOLUNTEER COMMITTEE! That's what it said on the sheet of paper pinned to the top of the board. HELP US MAKE THIS YEAR'S PLAY THE BEST ONE YET! SEE MS. FRIEDMAN BY 6/1/93 TO SIGN UP!

Slowly, McKinley squeezed shut her eyes. Harder and harder she squeezed, until pricks of light formed behind her eyelids. She took a deep breath and opened them again. Then she reread the paper.

Exactly the same. All the words were exactly the same. The date was the same, too.

6/1/93.

This wasn't some dream. She had no idea how it had happened, but it had.

McKinley O'Dair had definitely, without a doubt, somehow or other, traveled back in time.

6

Anytime You Need a Friend

*O*kay, McKinley thought, taking her deepest breath. In through her nose, out through her mouth. *This is not the worst thing that's ever happened.* In, out, in, out. *It's not like you got sucked back into the middle of a war or something.* In, out, in, out. *It's the '90s. They have cereal with sprinkles in it. You LOVE sprinkles.* In out in out. *Anyway, at least you know you won't be stuck here forever.* In-outinoutinoutinout. *Because you're going to FREAKING DIE FROM A FREAKING PANIC ATTACK FIRST.*

McKinley had to pull herself together. She needed help. Who could help her? Her dad? He was twelve. Meg? She wasn't born yet. Grandma Bev? What would McKinley tell her—"Hey, it's me, your future grandkid. Mind if I crash here while I *figure out how to FREAKING TIME TRAVEL?*"

Inoutinoutinoutinoutinoutinoutinout.

And then, suddenly, McKinley stopped hyperventilating. Just like that. She knew exactly who she could turn to.

If you ever need to talk, or need my help, you can come find me, anytime.

Anytime. That's what Jackie had told her.

Now McKinley just had to see if she'd meant it.

* * *

While she walked, McKinley worried. She'd seen enough movies to know that when someone had something unbelievable to say, they were going to get a door slammed in their face. Then they'd have to spend like an entire montage convincing the person that they were really telling the truth. And McKinley did not have an entire montage's worth of time to waste. She needed some fact that she *couldn't* know about twelve-year-old Jackie, but somehow did, so McKinley could convince her she was from the future.

Unfortunately, the only thing McKinley could think of was that Jackie had once exploded a Pop-Tart in the microwave. And that didn't seem like enough to convince anyone.

One block away from Meg's grandparents' house, McKinley's insides were twisted with worry. "Excuse me," she grumbled at the kid walking slow as a sloth in quicksand in front of her. The girl had a lime-green monkey key chain hanging off her backpack and was taking up half the sidewalk.

The kid didn't seem to hear. "*Excuse me,*" McKinley said again. There wasn't *quite* enough room to squeeze by. McKinley finally gave up and crossed into the street, darting around two parked cars and still making it back to the sidewalk before the girl caught up to her. When she glanced over her shoulder, McKinley saw that the girl had her nose buried deep in a book. Who *read* while they *walked*? She still hadn't even noticed McKinley.

McKinley made a beeline for the house on the corner. 1301

Spruce Lane—Meg's grandparents' house, the same one Jackie had grown up in. The shutters were red now instead of white, but otherwise it looked just as McKinley had always known it.

Here goes nothing, McKinley thought. She raised her fist. She knocked.

She waited.

McKinley knocked again.

She waited.

McKinley was just raising her fist to knock a *third* time when she heard someone clearing their throat behind her.

"Can I help you?" said a voice.

McKinley spun around.

It was the girl with the book. She was sucking on a lollipop, one finger stuck between the book's pages to mark her place, and she was staring at McKinley.

"What?" McKinley said, annoyed.

"I live here," the girl replied.

"Wait." McKinley tilted her head, taking the girl in. The wavy dark-brown hair with crooked bangs and split ends. The pale, freckly skin. "You're Jackie." It wasn't so much a question as a realization.

"Yup." Twelve-year-old Jackie twisted the lollipop around in her mouth. "Who're you?"

McKinley took the deepest of deep breaths. (When she got back to her own time, McKinley was going to have to inform her PE teacher that their meditation unit had really come in handy.) *Here goes nothing*, she thought.

"My name's McKinley," she said. "I'm best friends with your daughter, Meg. I traveled here from the year 2018, and I need your help." McKinley clenched her teeth and waited to be laughed off the doorstep.

Instead, Jackie reached right past McKinley and twisted open her front door. Then she grabbed McKinley's hand and dragged her inside. "Dad!" Jackie called to the man sitting in the living room, with his gaze so focused on his book that McKinley began to understand where Jackie got it from. "This is that foreign exchange student I told you about, remember? She's staying with us for a while. We're going to my room! Don't bug us! Bye!"

And Jackie's dad—who McKinley knew as Meg's spacey Papa Fritz—didn't even look up from his novel. "Oh, okay, right. Hi there."

"Uh, hi," McKinley said as Jackie dragged her deeper into the house.

When they reached what must've been Jackie's childhood bedroom, Jackie shut the door with a bang and practically threw herself on her bed. "Okay," she said, her hands in her lap as she stared up at McKinley. McKinley shifted from one foot to the other, trying to prepare herself for the grilling of her life. Her eyes darted around the room, taking in the *Saved by the Bell* poster, the mountains and mountains of books, and the tiny boxy TV with the built-in VCR. (*Be kind, rewind*, McKinley found herself thinking with a snort. She'd been rewound, all right.) But before she could figure out any way to explain things,

Jackie continued on. "Tell me *everything* about the future," Jackie said.

McKinley frowned. "Huh?" she replied.

Jackie chomped off the last of her lollipop and tossed the stick in the wastebasket. "You know, all the good stuff. Are there flying cars? How many novels have I written? Am I a super-famous writer, or only sort of famous? Is there world peace yet? What kind of dog do I have?" She reached under her pillow and pulled out a slim rectangular package of something called Dunkaroos. "Want some?" She peeled off the foil top.

"Uh, sure." McKinley sat down next to Jackie cautiously, taking one of the kangaroo-shaped cookies Jackie offered her. "Thanks." She dipped the cookie into the tiny square of frosting like Jackie did with hers. "But, um, don't you want me to, like, *prove* I'm from the future?"

Jackie bit the head off her own chocolate-haired kangaroo. "You already did," she said. And when McKinley raised her eyebrows, Jackie nodded toward the book between them on the bed, the one she'd been reading on the walk home. McKinley read the title. *A Wrinkle in Time.*

"I don't get it," McKinley said.

Jackie dunked two kangaroos at once. "It's my favorite book. You ever read it?" McKinley shook her head. "It's about a girl who time travels. And I decided like two years ago that if I ever had a daughter, I'd name her after the main character. Meg. Anyway"—Jackie tossed one kangaroo into her mouth, then the other—"how often does someone from the future show up on your doorstep and ask you for help? That'd be a super-weird thing to lie about." She offered McKinley another Dunkaroo. "What'd you say your name was again? Mickey?"

"McKinley."

"Well, whatever you need, McKinley, I'll help you out. We'll get you back to the future in no time. And don't worry about my dad," she added when McKinley's gaze drifted toward the door. "When my stepmom's on one of her business trips, I could tell him we signed up for father-daughter space travel and he'd believe me. I'm basically in charge the whole time Adelle's gone, and she's in Taipei for a month." Jackie offered McKinley another Dunkaroo.

"Thanks," McKinley said, taking the cookie. She felt like an enormous weight had been lifted off her shoulders. She'd definitely made the right decision in coming to Jackie. "It's pretty great to have a friend right now," she told her. "You have no idea."

But McKinley did wonder, as Jackie scooped out the last of the frosting with her finger, if Jackie would be *quite* so nice if she knew about the last conversation McKinley had had with her future daughter.

(*Olive loaf.* Why hadn't McKinley just *olive loaf*ed?)

Maybe it'd be best to leave out that little detail for now.

7

Break It Down Again

One thing was true about Jacqueline Yorks-one-day-to-be-Rothstein—even at twelve years old, she could make things *happen*. By the time McKinley had woken up, wearing a pair of Jackie's teal-and-pink-striped PJs, snuggled in Jackie's *Fresh Prince of Bel-Air* sleeping bag, Jackie had already forged enough documents to reenroll McKinley at her own school.

"Why do I need to go, though?" McKinley asked as they strode down the sidewalk. The air was crisp, and McKinley was wearing yet more borrowed stuff—jean shorts with rolled-up cuffs, a white tank top, and an oversize purple flannel that she'd tied around her waist. "You'd think if I had to time travel, at least I could get a vacation out of it."

"We have no idea how long you'll be here," Jackie replied. When she wasn't busy reading, Jackie was practically a turbo walker. McKinley had to walk at double speed to keep up. "And if you don't come to school with me, my dad might get suspicious."

McKinley wasn't so sure about that. At breakfast, Papa Fritz had looked up at McKinley, startled, and said, "Oh yeah, you're here! What's your name again?"

"I'm Mc—" McKinley had stopped herself just in time. What

if, in the future, Papa Fritz met her again and was like, "Wait a minute. There was a foreign exchange student named McKinley O'Dair twenty-five years ago who looked exactly like you."

"Mickey," she'd said at last, and Jackie had nodded excitedly, like the future editor in her couldn't wait to craft this fib into fiction gold.

"Mickey *Wells*," Jackie had added. (Later, Jackie explained, "You know, like H. G. Wells, the writer. Clever, huh?" And when McKinley had stared at her blankly, Jackie had puffed up her bangs with a sigh and explained, "He wrote *The Time Machine*?" McKinley had only shrugged.)

Papa Fritz nodded into his coffee. "Okay," he said. "I forgot to tell Adelle you arrived when she called last night, but I'll remember next week." McKinley wasn't so sure he would, but she planned on being long gone by then anyway.

Now, as she and Jackie sprinted to school, McKinley tried to take in the neighborhood. She'd seen it yesterday, of course, but she'd been too panicked to really notice much. Like the houses, here and there, painted different colors. Or the empty lot where the yoga studio had always stood. Tiny sprouts where there'd once been full, leafy trees. The most obvious difference was the cars—all boxy, less shiny. No SUVs anywhere. And there was the newspaper box on the corner, which McKinley was so fascinated by that Jackie finally gave her a quarter to put in, just to get McKinley moving again. Then they passed a telephone booth, which was even weirder. (Jackie still refused to believe McKinley that in the future even kids had cell phones.)

At last they turned the corner onto Canary Lane, and the school came into view.

"Anyway," Jackie went on, unaware that McKinley had totally forgotten they were having a conversation, "this is where you were when you time traveled, right? So if we're going to figure out how to get you back, we might as well start at the scene of the crime. Come on, we've only got like ten minutes before the bell rings."

The first place they investigated was the girls' bathroom. Since that's where McKinley had done her time traveling, Jackie thought there might be some sort of portal. The girls checked the sinks. They stood on the rims of the toilets and squinted at the ceiling. Jackie even put her ear to the wall and knocked on it (which as far as McKinley was concerned, just seemed unsanitary).

No portal.

"I don't think this is working," McKinley said while Jackie pumped all the soap out of the dispensers. The bell for homeroom had already rung, but McKinley wasn't so sad to be late. Somehow she'd ended up in Mr. Jones's homeroom *again*. Like once in a lifetime wasn't bad enough. "If there were a portal in here, don't you think someone besides us would've found it already?"

Jackie turned on the faucet to rinse the soap off her hand. "That's a good point," she said. "Maybe it's not *where* you were when you time traveled that's important. Maybe we should be thinking about *when*."

McKinley wrinkled her nose. "What do you mean? I traveled to now."

"No," Jackie said. "I mean . . ." She scrunched her mouth to the side, thinking. "In books, there's always an 'inciting incident.' Something that happens that starts the hero off on their journey. So if this were a book—"

"*McKinley's Stupendous Time-Travel Adventure?*" McKinley suggested.

Jackie grinned. "Perfect. If this were a book, then the thing that happened right before you went back would be important. It'd be, like . . . some sort of huge conflict. And before you could go back to your own time, you'd need to fix it. What?" she asked when she spotted McKinley's frown. "I told you, I took three creative writing classes at the Y last summer. I was the only person under forty." She paused and tilted her head to one side. "Are you *sure* I don't become a writer?"

McKinley shook her head. They'd already talked about this for about two hours last night. "But you love being an editor, I swear. You told me it's like being the boss of storytelling. *Anyway* . . . " McKinley tried to pull the focus back to the whole how-the-heck-do-I-get-home issue. "Do you really think I have to solve some big problem before I can go back? Because that's kind of terrifying. How am I supposed to solve a problem if I have no idea what the problem is?" McKinley was going to be stuck in the '90s forever.

"Don't worry, we've got this," Jackie told her. "Just walk me through exactly what happened before I pushed you into the bathroom."

McKinley bit her lip, trying to remember all the details. "Like I said, I brought Grandma Bev to the Time Hop, and we looked around for a bit." McKinley missed Grandma Bev already. Was she okay? Had someone given her her meds? Would McKinley ever get to see her again? "I signed in for the fashion show. I . . ." McKinley darted her eyes toward Jackie. She didn't need to mention the fight with Meg, she decided. It wasn't like *that* was a problem she could solve right now anyway. "I went onstage." (But what if McKinley never saw Meg again? What if the last thing Meg ever remembered about her was their fight and that McKinley *could've* said "olive loaf" but she didn't? McKinley hated the idea that she could simply vanish from her own time, leaving Meg to hate her forever.) "And my dad was a giant jerk and embarrassed me in front of the entire town, and then I bolted off the stage and ran into you, and you hid me in here. Oh, and you locked Mr. Jones in a closet. But I told you that already."

Jackie's grin took over her whole face. "Yeah," she said. "I really like that part. Mr. Jones is the worst."

"The *absolute* worst," McKinley agreed. "Anyway, the next thing I knew, I found my own dad as a sixth grader, and the rest is kind of a blur."

Jackie was rolling something around in her mouth. "Want one?" she asked, holding out an open package of Warheads candy.

McKinley shook her head. Where had that even come from? "It's like 7:30 in the morning," she said.

Jackie only shrugged. She slid the candy across her tongue, thinking. McKinley left her to it.

"All right," Jackie said at last. "It seems like the fashion show was the site of your main conflict. Which means that what happened on that stage in the gym is central to your story arc." McKinley nodded. It made as much sense as anything she'd come up with. "So," Jackie went on, "that's where we should go next."

They left the bathroom just as the bell for first period rang, Jackie leading the way. McKinley was more than happy to follow.

At least *someone* had a plan.

8

Whoops Now

The gymnasium of Gap Bend Public School had never looked less like the setting for a Time Hop. Stacks of wrestling mats dominated one wall, a rolling bin of basketballs sat askew in a corner. Near the stage was a giant carved wooden statue of Gregory Groundhog, the GBPS mascot, with a sign around his narrow groundhog neck reading DON'T TOUCH ME! I'M FRAGILE! (The statue was pretty cute actually, with its huge buckteeth. McKinley wondered why she'd never seen it in her own time.)

"Okay, so this is good because technically we have PE right now anyway," Jackie said, dragging McKinley across the floor. Other kids were racing to the locker rooms to put on their gym clothes, but Jackie was steering them to the opposite side. "But if Miss Cho asks why we haven't changed yet, I'll just tell her I'm giving you a tour, 'kay?"

McKinley nodded. She could already tell that Jackie was the boss of their friendship, and she was fine with it. It felt good right now, letting someone take care of her.

"Now," Jackie went on, "when we get backstage, I need you to try to remember every single detail from the fashion show. You never know what might be the key to figuring out what you need to change, so use all your senses to bring you back to that moment—every sight, sound, touch, smell, taste . . . Well, maybe not ta—*oof!*"

Jackie suddenly smacked into the ground, hard. "Hey!" she cried. "Excuse you!"

Meanwhile, the kid who'd run backward into her clearly didn't feel too bad about it. "Look where you're going, four eyes!" he snapped back.

McKinley did a double take.

The kid was her dad.

Jackie brushed some gym floor off her elbow as she rose to her feet. "You know that insult only works if the person you're insulting wears glasses, right, Billy?" she called to him.

"Let's go, 'kay?" McKinley told Jackie. She was still weirded out being so close to the twelve-year-old version of her dad. "We have work to do."

Billy tossed his basketball from one hand to the other. "Maybe you should *get* glasses," he replied, just as Kid Ron jogged up to join him. McKinley felt like she was in the middle of a weirdness sandwich. "Then you'd be able to see how ugly you are."

"What?" McKinley said. Had her father seriously just called Jackie *ugly*? "You *know* if I said something like that, you'd . . ." She trailed off, realizing she really shouldn't finish her sentence.

"Yeah, B, that was kind of low, actually." This came from Ron, who scrunched up his nose like he hated to call out a fellow bro. (McKinley knew her dad and Ron had been friends since they were young—she'd always assumed that her dad was such a nerd that Ron had befriended him out of pity.)

But Jackie didn't seem at all fazed by the insult. "At least I don't need glasses to see how stupid you are, Billy."

"Seriously?" McKinley said, her neck twinging at the awful word. What was with all the insults? Her dad and Jackie sure hadn't behaved this way when they were co-chairing PTO Bingo Night.

"You're so stupid," Jackie went on (McKinley's neck twinged again), "you'd need *two* pairs of—"

Wham!

Billy's basketball hit Jackie right in the forehead.

"Ow!" Jackie screeched.

And McKinley was *furious*.

"Why are you guys acting like such jerks?" she screamed, snatching the basketball from its rebound arc. And she chucked it with angry force across the room, so these two bozos who'd both once bandaged her boo-boos could no longer use it to pummel each other.

Unfortunately, despite years of PE evidence that would suggest otherwise, McKinley was apparently a super-strong ball thrower . . . and a super-unlucky aimer. Because without meaning to at all, McKinley had sent the basketball careening—*WHAM!*—right into Gregory Groundhog's fat head. With a sickening *CRACK!* poor Gregory's head snapped right off its neck and rolled across the gym floor, every student in the room staring in disbelief as it went. And it didn't stop rolling until it reached the gym entrance. There, its big round groundhog eyes fixed on McKinley as though to say, *What did I ever do to you?*

McKinley's whole face burned. She was a groundhog murderer. A time-traveling groundhog murderer.

And as it happened, she wasn't the only person shaken up about it.

"You again!"

The voice belonged to (just McKinley's luck) none other than Mr. Jones. He stepped over Gregory Groundhog's dismembered head and stormed toward her, rage glistening in his eyes. Even Miss Cho, the gym teacher, stepped out of his way. "That's two incidents of vandalism this week from you four!" he spat.

"Uh, four?" McKinley asked. She wasn't sure what else to say. Her knees were shaking. How was it that Mr. Jones managed to witness all her worst moments?

"Four," Mr. Jones repeated, and he pointed to his culprits. "One, two, three, four."

McKinley, Jackie, Billy, and Ron.

"But that's not fair!" Billy whined. "Me and Ronny didn't do anything to that stupid groundhog! It was her!" He was pointing at McKinley.

McKinley narrowed her eyes at him. "Way to throw me under the bus," she said. Leave it to William O'Dair Jr. to go and narc on his own daughter.

Billy narrowed his eyes right back. "Who even *are* you?" he replied.

"She's Mickey Wells," Jackie told him. "She's new."

Ronny leaned across Billy to wave. "Hi, Mickey," he said cheerfully.

"Uh . . ." McKinley wasn't sure where to turn her head. "Hi?"

Mr. Jones was clearly not done being angry. "Yes," he said dryly. "Hello, Mickey. Welcome to Gap Bend. As your very first activity, you'll be joining your friends here in after-school detention."

"What?" all four kids shrieked together.

Mr. Jones somehow looked even scarier with his new head of hair. "That," he told them, "is the punishment for vandalism."

"That wasn't vandalism," Jackie argued, pointing to Gregory's head (which two kids had already turned into a soccer ball). "It was an accident."

"Miss Yorks," Mr. Jones said, turning his pointy nose toward her. "Was it or was it not *your* rocket that spewed seltzer all over the girls' bathroom yesterday?"

"That was my science project," Jackie argued. "Billy *stole* it!"

McKinley threw up her hands in the air at that. "Seriously?" she asked Billy again. "You stole her science project?"

It was clear Billy wanted to respond to that, but Mr. Jones cut him off with a death glare. "All four of you," he told them, "will be in the library at two thirty sharp this afternoon. And if I were you, I'd cancel any plans you have for next week as well."

"All next week?" Billy screeched. "You can't make us—"

"You're lucky I don't make you clean toilets," Mr. Jones said. "But as it happens, Ms. Friedman needs some help with the Time Hop play, and I promised her I'd find some able volunteers." He eyed each of them in turn. "You all look quite able to me."

And that, as it turned out, was that.

9

All You Have to Do

Ugh, sorry you had to deal with that back there," Jackie said to McKinley as they hustled to the girls' locker room to change. Miss Cho was keeping a careful eye on them this time. "That Billy kid is the worst. Like, the actual worst human on the planet. I've been stuck dealing with him my whole life, because my dad and his mom got this idea in their heads that just because we both had parents who died, we should be best friends. Like, that is *so* not how it works, m'kay? But they used to send me over to his house to hang out nearly every day after school anyway. And he is the worst, McKinley, you have no idea. One time when we were six, he chopped off all my hair with a pair of kid scissors because he said I acted so much like a boy I should look like one, too."

"Wait, wh-what?" McKinley stammered. This was the first she'd heard any of this.

"Yeah. I guess in Billy's idiot brain" —McKinley's neck twinged again at Jackie's unfortunate word choice, but she decided to let it go, considering—"girls shouldn't be better than him at Crazy Eights or whatever. I had, like, the *most* unfortunate mushroom haircut until halfway through second grade. Anyway, the point is"—Jackie took a long overdue gulp of air—"just because I have to deal with that moron"—(*twinge*)—"doesn't mean you should have to, too. I'll find some way to get us out of detention, don't worry. Then we can focus on figuring out what problem you need to fix, and you'll be on your way home, and you'll never have to see stupid Billy O'Dair ever again."

(Twinge, twinge.)

"Uh."

McKinley stopped walking. It took a few steps for Jackie to realize, but then she stopped, too. Backtracked. She looked at McKinley expectantly.

"Didn't I tell you last night?" McKinley said. She could've sworn she had. But there were so very many topics to cover after you time traveled, and she'd been so very tired . . .

"Tell me what?" Jackie asked.

"Billy," McKinley replied. "He's my dad."

For the second time that morning, Jackie nearly toppled over. *"What?"* Jackie clearly could not believe it. *"He's* your dad? I'm so sorry, McKinley. Jeez. He's the worst! Like, the actual worst human on—"

"On the planet," McKinley finished for her. "You mentioned. And you should really quit saying 'stupid' and stuff. It's not—"

But Jackie had stopped listening. "No wonder you tried to take his head off with a basketball," she said.

"I wasn't trying to—"

"Believe me, I get it," Jackie assured her. "If Billy was my dad, I'd break the laws of physics just to get away from him, too. Too bad you couldn't've traveled to an alternate timeline where Billy never existed. I bet that timeline is *amazing.*"

And even though there was a small part of McKinley that

agreed, she wasn't sure how she felt about someone else saying so out loud. Especially if that someone else was once on a two-year-long group chat about soccer snacks with the person she wanted to wipe from time. But Miss Cho hollered at them to get a move on, and then she assigned McKinley a gym locker six rows away from Jackie's, so that was the end of the conversation.

It wasn't until they were running dribble relays on the court that Jackie tried to talk to McKinley again. Unfortunately, she was only able to huff out a few words at a time as she and McKinley passed each other the basketball in between sprints.

"I figured out . . ." Jackie said as McKinley grabbed the ball. McKinley took off for the cone across the court, dribbling and running as fast as she could. "What you need to do . . ." Jackie continued before grabbing the ball back and sprinting off again. The gym echoed with squeaks and shrieks. "To get back . . ." Jackie went on. McKinley ran and dribbled. "To your own time." *Huff huff huff huff.* Jackie was out of breath now, and she nearly tripped on her way around the cone. "The thing you need to change is . . ." McKinley took off with the ball, her heart soaring with hope for the first time all day. (Had Jackie really figured it out? Was there really a way for McKinley to go home?) McKinley shot the ball into Jackie's hands with a *thwack!* just as Jackie finally finished her thought.

"Your dad."

The more McKinley thought about what Jackie had said, the more it made sense. Of *course* the problem was her dad. His horrible "system" and the way he'd embarrassed her during the fashion show—that was what had set this whole time-travel thing into motion. As Jackie explained as they chomped on tater tots during lunch, "Every story has an obstacle. Some problem that keeps the main character from getting what they want. And in *McKinley's Stupendous Time-Travel Adventure*, that problem is your dad. So if you want to go home, you have to figure out how to fix it. To fix *him*."

Well, if this was the universe's way of telling McKinley that her dad needed a total makeover, she was there for it. And fortunately, McKinley knew a thing or two about how to get a person to change.

"Connie's C.R.A.B.S. change lives!" McKinley declared, setting down her carton of chocolate milk with a slosh.

"Hold on, hold on," Jackie said as McKinley began explaining the five steps of Aunt Connie's C.R.A.B.S. method. "I gotta write this down." She pulled out a spiral notebook with a picture of Garfield the cat on the cover. Underneath Garfield, in permanent marker, she'd scribbled *Jackie's Stories!!!!* She flicked past page after page filled up with her loopy, sloppy writing, until she found a clean sheet. Then she copied down the steps of C.R.A.B.S., just as McKinley explained them (with a tiny bit of her own personal flair).

How to Make Billy Not So Terrible

Step #1: COUNT his blessings.

Step #2: RIGHT his wrongs.

Step #3: ASSESS his neighbors.

Step #4: BETTER his world.

Step #5: SHAKE up his routine.

Easy peasy, McKinley thought. She'd be zooming back to 2018 before her dad even realized he was being improved. Suddenly, McKinley was glad she'd gotten sucked into the past. Thrilled, even. Who else got a chance to fix the biggest problem in their life before it even began? When McKinley returned, she'd be living with Dad 2.0. He wouldn't be so glued to his "system," McKinley could enter any fashion show she wanted, and they'd be able to order a pizza on a whim without her dad melting down about it. Best of all, there would no longer be anyone stopping McKinley from being *her*.

"Let's make Billy extra crabby!" Jackie announced as she slapped her notebook shut.

10

Human Behaviour

As it turned out, getting thrown into detention was the best thing that could've happened to McKinley. A perfect opportunity to get started on her plan.

As soon as she and Jackie stepped into the library after school, McKinley made a beeline for the table where Billy and Ronny were sitting.

"Ugh," Jackie whined as McKinley dragged her across the library. "I'd rather sit next to a man-eating python."

In reply, McKinley gave her the Connie's C.R.A.B.S. salute—two quick claw snaps with both hands. Jackie let out a loud huff of irritation. But she followed.

Of course, as soon as they sat down, Billy scooched his chair across the floor as loudly and as far away as possible—like *she* was the man-eating python.

"Real mature," McKinley muttered.

At the front of the room, Ms. Friedman clapped her hands together. "Let's get down to business," she said. "We have four new volunteers to welcome." She pointed to McKinley's table. "We're so glad you're here."

"Us, too!" Billy shouted. Then he tugged down on his bottom eyelids with his eyes rolled back in his head.

Seriously, *this* was the guy who was always on McKinley's case about "acting her age"?

"As you know," Ms. Friedman went on, "we only have eight days until the Time Hop and only seven until we perform the play at the school-wide assembly. We need to have the play written, scored, and costumed by then, and everyone needs to have all their lines memorized as well. And since half of our committee recently lost their extracurricular privileges because of the Great Sour Punch Straws Scandal of Ninety-Three"—McKinley could tell there was a whole 'nother story there, but now didn't exactly seem like the time to ask about it—"we're in a real pickle, frankly."

The other six members of the Time Hop volunteer committee may have cared deeply about the pickle they were in, but clearly no one at McKinley's table did.

"Ooh, is that a new story you're working on?" Ron whispered, grabbing the Garfield notebook Jackie had pulled out of her backpack. "Can I read it?"

McKinley stretched her whole body across the table to snatch it away. "Give it back!" she cried. Her face was hot with panic. What if Billy saw that they were crabbifying him? "You and Billy aren't allowed to read it!"

"Oh, don't worry," Jackie said, taking the notebook back from McKinley. She didn't seem stressed in the slightest. "Billy couldn't read it anyway. It's higher than reading-level one."

"Hey," McKinley said as the twinge in her neck started back up again. She knew Jackie couldn't stand her dad—and she got it—but poking fun at his reading just seemed low. She turned to Billy and noticed his hurt face, dark like a storm cloud. But then he noticed her noticing and flicked her in the arm. "Ow!" she cried.

Ms. Friedman clapped her hands again. "Excuse me!" she shouted. "Do we have a problem over there?"

"*No*," McKinley, Jackie, Billy, and Ron all muttered together.

"Good," Ms. Friedman replied. "Now, as I was saying, we've got music, props, and choreography for the play pretty well covered, but there's *no one* on costumes anymore, and Chanel could definitely use some help with the script."

McKinley's hand shot into the air. "I'll do costumes!" she shouted. This was perfect. "Billy can help, too! We both know how to sew!"

Billy's eyes went wide. "What?" he cried. "No I don't!"

But McKinley wasn't about to let this opportunity slip through her fingers. Working together on costumes every day for the next eight days would give McKinley *tons* of time to crabbify her father.

"He can, too," McKinley told Ms. Friedman. "His mom taught him when he was five." McKinley knew that for a fact because her dad had told her once that instead of an allowance, Grandma Bev used to pay him a dollar a hem to help with her tailoring.

There were snickers from a few kids around the room, but Ms. Friedman silenced them all with a glare. "Wonderful," she said. "You two set up in the corner over there. That box has everything the Sour Straw Seven left us for costumes. And that leaves you"—she pointed to Jackie and Ron—"on script-writing duty."

"But—" Jackie began, darting eyes at Ron.

"But—" Billy started, glowering at McKinley.

"Let's get to it!" Ms. Friedman replied. And that was that.

"I can't believe you told everyone I know how to sew," Billy grumbled, flicking a paper football across the library table. "How'd you even know that, anyway? I never told anyone."

McKinley dug her arm deeper into the costume box and pulled out another mound of useless items. A paisley muumuu, a pair of binoculars, and a dinosaur mask. The theme for the Time Hop this year was 1939, and their budget for costumes was— according to Ms. Friedman—"less than zero." No wonder Ms. Friedman had asked for help.

"Well, clearly you told *someone*," McKinley answered Billy, "or else how would I know about it?"

Apparently Billy couldn't think of a good argument for that, because he only grumbled louder.

"Anyway," McKinley went on, pulling a giant green tablecloth out of the box. "I don't know why you care so much if people know you can sew. Sewing is awesome. I love it."

Billy didn't look up from his one-man football game. "Big shock," he said. "Sewing's dumb and you're dumb, too."

Anger rose up in McKinley's throat. "Right," she said. She

wasn't even going to begin trying to school her dad about his ableist language. Clearly he wouldn't get it. "Just because *I* love to do something, you automatically think it's not worth doing."

Billy's football shot off at a bad angle, landing—*plop!*—in the costume box. When he looked up at McKinley, he had one eyebrow raised.

"You're a weird person," he told her.

McKinley swallowed down her anger. Anger wouldn't change her dad. "Are you gonna help me look through this stuff or not?" she asked him. (So, okay, maybe she hadn't swallowed down *all* the anger.)

To McKinley's shock, Billy actually got up from his seat. He walked over to the box, and he peered inside.

Then he plucked out his paper football and returned to the table.

"Not," he said.

McKinley took a deep breath. *Calm*, she told herself. *Stay calm. Not angry.* She needed to focus on step one—getting Billy to count his blessings.

"So," McKinley started, plopping another pile of items onto the table. A cheerleader skirt, a pair of parachute pants, an old doll hat . . . "Did you ever think about all the amazing—"

Billy interrupted her by scooching his chair back from the table with a loud *fruuuuuump!* "I'm gonna go to the bathroom," he said. "Have fun with all of this."

It looked like *someone* wasn't going to make this whole crab thing so easy peasy after all.

11

What Is Love

McKinley had just finished sorting through all the costumes—useless, useless, and more useless—when she heard a loud *Psssst!* from behind her. Jackie was in the corner with the weird boxy gray computers. She jerked her head for McKinley to come join her.

"What's up?" McKinley asked when she got to Jackie.

"*Shhh!*" Jackie whispered. She was turning the crank on a wall-mounted pencil sharpener. "Pretend you're looking through the card catalog." She gestured with one shoulder to the large wooden chest of drawers beside her.

"Oh . . . *kay*," McKinley said slowly. She turned to the card catalog and pulled open one of the long, long drawers. Inside were hundreds of cream-colored cards that looked like they'd been typed on with an *actual typewriter*. "Whoa," she breathed. "This is so retro."

Jackie sharpened faster. "Focus," she told McKinley. "Ms. Friedman is gonna notice us any minute. I just had to get away from Ronny. How's the crabbing going?"

"Well, Billy's been in the bathroom for the past twenty minutes, so . . ." McKinley flipped through the cards with a sigh. "It's sort of . . . not? Going, I mean." How was she ever supposed to get back to her own timeline if she couldn't even get her dad to talk to her for three straight seconds? She missed Grandma Bev. She missed her bedroom. And her sewing machine. And her phone.

And Meg. She missed Meg more than she wanted to think about.

Jackie nodded. "Well, I have some good news, anyway. Ms. Friedman said I can use the microfiche machine to look up articles from 1939 for the script. I figure when no one's looking, I can search for stuff on Billy. Something you can use to help crabbify him."

That's when McKinley made Jackie explain what a microfiche machine was, and that took a while. Apparently, it was some sort of microscope-like gizmo that you could use to read, like, any newspaper since the dawn of time. It sounded like the internet, only slower and without videos. But for whatever reason, Jackie was super stoked about it.

"The librarian *never* lets sixth graders use it," she explained, sharpening her pencil down to a stump. "It's so cool! And there's stuff in the *Gap Bend Gazette* on everyone, so I'm sure I'll get something on Billy. If we can figure out what 'wrongs' he needs to 'right,' he'll be halfway crabbed. Maybe I'll check the police blotter first. I bet he robbed an Utz truck when he was seven or something."

McKinley snorted. Her dad was annoying, sure, but he didn't exactly seem like a potato chip thief.

Just as Jackie inserted a new pencil into the sharpener, McKinley spotted Billy slipping through the library door.

"I better get back to my table," she told Jackie.

"Oh, please hang out with me for one more minute," Jackie begged. "Ronny's decided he's going to come up with fifty different words for fart, and when I left he was on 'stink shooter.' Please tell me that in the future Little Ronny Rothstein gets eaten by a polar bear or something."

"Uh . . ." McKinley began. How had she not told Jackie about Ron yet?

"You have to tell me." Jackie was spinning the pencil crank faster than ever. "It's no fair you know the future and I don't."

"Well . . ." McKinley rubbed the back of her neck.

"Ooh! Is it a carnival-ride accident? Is that how he bites it? Or, like, he eats too many Kandy Kakes and his stomach explodes? I know it's gotta be something ridiculous."

McKinley took a deep breath.

"He . . ."

"Yeah?"

"He . . . marries you," McKinley said at last.

The *crack!* of the pencil inside the sharpener let McKinley know exactly how Jackie felt about *that* news.

"You guys are totally in love," McKinley said quickly, trying to be encouraging. "And you have Meg, and she's awesome. I swear, you're super happy."

Once, years ago, McKinley had left a bunch of broccoli boiling on the stove too long, and when she'd plucked out the florets, the liquid that was left behind was a sickly, watery green.

That was the color of Jackie's face now.

"I'm gonna puke," Jackie said.

"Everything all right over here?"

It was Ms. Friedman. "I think that pencil is sharp enough now, Jackie," she said. "Back to your groups, please."

Jackie would come around eventually, McKinley reasoned as she headed back to her seat. No matter how much they seemed to dislike each other now, Jackie and Ron were meant to be. McKinley turned her head just in time to see Jackie rip a piece of Scotch tape off a roll and slap it onto Ron's face, taping his mouth shut.

"What's wrong with you?" Billy asked as McKinley stumbled belly-first into a library chair. "Forgot how eyeballs work?"

McKinley pulled her focus back to her dad. Jackie and Ron would work themselves out. Meanwhile, *she* had real work to do.

"Your mom has a sewing machine, right?" McKinley asked Billy. She knew the answer already, but she waited for him to nod anyway. "Good. I'm coming over to your house after this. We have a lot of work to do if we're going to finish these costumes by next Friday." And before Billy could argue, McKinley added, "Unless you want me to tell Ms. Friedman you're not being helpful? I'm sure Mr. Jones would be happy to find another sort of detention for you. I think he said something about toilets . . ."

"I can't stand you," Billy said. Which McKinley knew meant she'd won.

"Right back at you," McKinley replied.

It was time to stop messing around.

12

Come to My Window

Climbing the steps to the house with the yellow door on 536 Minnow Road, McKinley felt like Alice must've after she stepped through the looking glass. It was McKinley's house—the same house she'd held her mermaid-themed seventh birthday party in and broken her arm playing Floor Is Lava with Meg in and learned to sew with Grandma Bev in—but at the same time, it wasn't. The two pots with the pansies were missing, for one thing. The chip in the railing from when she'd dragged her wagon up the steps when she was five had been fixed. Or, rather, it hadn't needed to be fixed yet. And there were curtains inside the windows instead of blinds.

"Bev!" Suddenly there was a voice from inside the house. "There's some weird girl peeking in through your windows!" It was Aunt Connie. "I think she's casing the joint!"

A moment later, the door flew open, and there was Grandma Bev, standing before McKinley. *Standing*. Tall, with broad shoulders, short-cropped red hair, and a simple but smart blue dress with a wide pointed collar. Completely different from the Grandma Bev McKinley had always known—and yet so familiar. Without thinking, McKinley took a step forward and wrapped up her grandmother in an enormous hug. McKinley hadn't quite realized, until just that moment, how terribly she'd missed her.

After a few seconds of being squeezed, Grandma Bev gently patted McKinley and pulled herself out of the hug. "Well!" she said. "May I ask what I did to deserve that?" Her words came out clean. Her smile was even, both sides of her mouth turned up just the same.

"I . . ." McKinley said slowly. Her grandmother must think she was a total whackadoo. Who went around hugging strangers? "Sorry." She tugged at the straps of the purple JanSport backpack she'd been borrowing from Jackie. "I didn't mean . . . Um, is Billy here?"

Grandma Bev shook her head. "Nope," she said. "Out wreaking havoc, probably. Want me to give him a message?"

"I . . . But . . ." McKinley could feel her mouth flapping open and closed like a fish pulled from the ocean. "But we're supposed to work on costumes for the Time Hop play. We're on the volunteer committee together. He said he'd be here."

"That sounds like Billy, all right," Grandma Bev replied. "I'm assuming his joining the volunteer committee wasn't exactly . . . voluntary?"

McKinley cleared her throat. "Um, no," she said.

And to McKinley's surprise, Grandma Bev let out a guffaw. It was definitely not how her dad would react if he found out McKinley had gotten into trouble at school.

"I guess I'll come back later," McKinley said. Stood up by her own father. "It was nice, uh, meeting you." So much for getting

Billy started on counting his blessings tonight. She'd have to crabbify extra hard tomorrow.

"Nonsense," Grandma Bev said, and she swung the door open wide. "Come on in. There are costumes to make!"

"But—"

That's when Aunt Connie appeared behind Grandma Bev with her hands on her hips. "Who's the kid?" she asked.

The Aunt Connie of decades ago looked eerily the same as the one McKinley had grown up knowing. Slender, with veiny arms and hair that was already well on its way to gray. She was wearing denim jean cutoffs that were shorter than even McKinley was allowed to wear and a balloon-big yellow knitted sweater with the sleeves rolled up.

Grandma Bev gently tugged McKinley into the house. "This is a friend of Billy's," she said, and she placed one hand on McKinley's shoulder as she introduced her. It was all McKinley could do to stop herself from reaching up to grab her hand and squeeze it. "They're working on a project together, and Billy stood her up."

"Sounds like Billy," Aunt Connie said. "What's her name?" She asked that to Grandma Bev, not McKinley.

"Didn't ask her yet," Grandma Bev replied.

"Bev." Aunt Connie put on her Very Serious Face. "You invited someone into your house without even knowing her name? How do you know she's not a cat burglar?"

Grandma Bev shifted to get a better look at McKinley's face. "Are you a cat burglar?" she asked.

McKinley had always known that Grandma Bev was funny, but now that she could get her words out exactly the way she wanted, it turned out she was sharp, too. *Quick.*

"Nope," McKinley told her.

"She says she's not," Grandma Bev told Aunt Connie, who only harrumphed.

"My name's Mickey," McKinley told them. "Mickey Wells. I'm new."

"Nice to meet you, Mickey," Grandma Bev said. "Just grab a seat wherever, and we'll get to work in a moment."

"We?" McKinley asked.

"Of course!" Grandma Bev seemed surprised McKinley had even asked. "Just because my son left you in the lurch doesn't mean I'm going to." McKinley made a mental note to put *Amazing Mother* at the very top of Billy's count-your-blessings list. "Connie," Grandma Bev went on, "I'm afraid I'm going to have to catch up with you later."

"Bev, really!"

"Sorry," Grandma Bev said with a shrug. "I have a cat burglar to help."

Aunt Connie let out a huff, but she caved in just as she always did with Grandma Bev. "Fine," she said, "but I'm bringing you a casserole tomorrow. That boy's getting way too skinny, and I know you haven't had time to cook in ages."

"I suppose I can live with that," Grandma Bev replied.

Second on the count-your-blessings list, McKinley realized, watching the two friends hug at the door, was *Aunt Connie*. She clearly loved Billy just as if he were her own kid. He was lucky to have her.

As Grandma Bev hustled Aunt Connie out the door, McKinley looked around for a place to sit down. If the outside of the house had given McKinley *Alice in Wonderland* vibes, the inside was maybe the *Stranger Things* Upside Down version of the house she was used to. The normally pristine living room was in shambles. One couch was covered in piles of folded laundry, with a small section reserved for an overflowing sewing box, and the coffee table was home to several tailoring projects midwork. The carpet looked like it hadn't been vacuumed since it was installed. The dining area was in chaos, too, with piles of all sorts—fabric, newspapers, books—stacked on the table, and the fancy china cabinet was stuffed with more odds and ends than plates and cups. In one glance, McKinley spied a flashlight, a globe, a paperweight, a box of toothpicks, and a stuffed triceratops. When McKinley craned her neck to look into the kitchen, she spotted a sink overflowing with dishes, cupboards left open, and a broom leaning against the oven with its dustpan on the floor. The grown-up version of her dad would've had convulsions just standing there.

Still, not everyone had a house to live in, messy or not. McKinley put *Great Place to Live* at number three on the list.

McKinley made her way to the familiar corner with the two sewing machines. One was her grandmother's old workhorse, but the other was different from the one McKinley remembered. It was pale blue and slightly smaller than normal, a kid-size version. McKinley wondered if this was the machine her dad had learned to sew on. She scooped up the pair of trousers that were folded on the seat in front of it so she could sit down, but two pins fell out of the hem. She got down on her hands and knees to dig them out of the carpet.

Grandma Bev made her way over to McKinley and crouched down to help. "So. What exactly are we working on?" she asked as they ran their hands carefully over the carpet to find the missing pins.

McKinley plucked the last pin from the floor. "You sure you want to help?" she said. She handed over the pin.

"Of course." Grandma Bev found the pair of trousers and re-inserted the pins properly, then made quick work of tidying up her sewing table while McKinley plopped herself down in a chair. "The Time Hop needs a play, and a play needs costumes. And God knows Billy's not gonna do it. I mean, I love that kid with my whole heart, but he's a bit of a punk, hmm?" McKinley decided it was best not to answer that. "Anyway, I owe you one for getting Connie out of my house before she reorganized my utensil drawer." McKinley laughed. Who knew Grandma Bev had been keeping such snarky thoughts inside her brain? "So"— she nodded to the stuffed backpack at McKinley's feet—"what are we working on?"

This was where McKinley might lose her. "We have to make a *Gone with the Wind* dress"—McKinley unzipped her backpack and pulled out the only thing in Ms. Friedman's Box of Rejects that would even remotely work—"out of this."

For a moment, Grandma Bev said nothing. Just stared at the ugly green padded tablecloth in McKinley's hands. She opened her mouth. Then closed it again.

At last she said, "Well, if Scarlett O'Hara can make a dress out of curtains, I suppose we can make one out of a tablecloth."

McKinley smiled. Same old Grandma Bev. "Awesome." She pulled out the sketches crammed at the bottom of the bag. "Here's what I was thinking," she said, doing her best to unwrinkle the pages against the tabletop. "I mean, if you ignore the fact that *Gone with the Wind* is kind of a dumpster fire of a movie that should probably be canceled"—Meg's Nana Adelle had suggested they watch it once, and afterward they'd all agreed that the film's take on Civil War politics were . . . problematic—"the costumes are pretty great. This one needs to fit this girl Chanel. I took her measurements . . ." McKinley found the paper with her scratchy scribbles on it. "Here. Anyway, don't worry, 'cause I'm already getting Jackie to fix the script for the play where they talk about it."

"You designed these?" Grandma Bev asked, flipping from one paper to the next. She let out a whistle McKinley had never known she could make.

McKinley nodded. "Ms. Friedman had some books for me to look at."

"These are fantastic." Grandma Bev glanced at the measurements next. "And you took arm length and outseam and everything? How'd you know to do all this?"

McKinley rubbed her hands on her shorts. "My grandma taught me," she said softly.

Grandma Bev nodded in approval. "Well, she must be a pretty spectacular lady," she said.

And in reply, McKinley told her grandmother what she probably should've said years and years ago.

"She is," she told her.

13

Someday I Suppose

At last Grandma Bev took a seat beside McKinley, and McKinley let out a breath of air she must've been holding for the past day and a half. *This*, right here—sitting beside Grandma Bev, in front of their two sewing machines—this felt right.

Within minutes, they were hard at work. McKinley did her best to take in everything—the way Grandma Bev's two hands, so agile and young and quick and smooth, worked the machine. The way she blew at a strand of her hair when it fell in her eyes while she was sewing. The smell of her shampoo. The sound of her humming. The slope of her shoulders as she cut out a piece of fabric. McKinley didn't want to forget a thing.

"The volunteer committee is lucky to have you," Grandma Bev told McKinley at one point. "And you're lucky, too—your first Time Hop? Now, that's something spectacular."

"Yeah," McKinley agreed. "It is. I mean, I bet it will be. Can't wait to see it."

That was item four on the count-your-blessings list, McKinley realized. This very town—*Gap Bend, Pennsylvania*—with its awesome people and awesome traditions. Billy had blessings practically spilling out of his ears.

They stitched and stitched. McKinley could not believe how incredibly *fast* Grandma Bev was.

"You could be in the Olympics or something," McKinley said. "Speed sewing."

Grandma Bev laughed. "Oh, if only that were a sport!" she said. "I would go pro in a heartbeat."

McKinley thought about that. "How come you never did?" she asked. "Go pro. I mean, I know you take in tailoring on the weekends, but . . ." She trailed off when she saw Grandma Bev's look of surprise. "Sorry, I didn't mean to pry. Billy was telling me you did that."

"No apology necessary," Grandma Bev replied. "I was just shocked my son said more than five words to you. But to answer your question, I am going to open up a full-time tailoring business soon. I've been taking business classes at night, keeping my eye on studio spaces in town. Should happen in the next few years."

"Really?" McKinley hadn't known that, about her grandmother's plans. Her heart swelled with happy pride . . . until, just as quickly, it deflated, when she realized why those plans never came to anything. Because, of course, it was much harder to own your own tailoring business after you'd had a stroke that left half your body paralyzed.

"You okay?" Grandma Bev asked, blinking at McKinley.

McKinley's throat had gone dry. Grandma Bev's stroke—it was going to happen soon, wasn't it? How many years of talking and walking did Grandma Bev have left? Two? Three? "I think you should do it soon," McKinley told her grandmother. "Don't even wait a second. Open your business now. Next week, even. I can help you, if you want. While I'm here, I mean." Who said Billy's was the only life McKinley should be improving while she was here? "I bet Billy would help you, too, if he knew . . . if he got how important it was. I'll tell him he should help you."

Grandma Bev smiled her two-sided smile. "Now, that's the kind of ambition I like to hear," she said. "I like you, Mickey. I'm glad you and Billy are becoming friends."

"Oh, we're not . . ." McKinley trailed off. Maybe Grandma Bev didn't need to know how aggravating McKinley found her son to be, now and in the future. "Uh, I think he's really good friends with Ron, though?"

"Yeah, Ronny's a good egg," Grandma Bev said. She pulled a pin out of the length of tablecloth skirt she was about to sew over. "I think he and Billy balance each other pretty well."

And that was item number five. *Awesome Best Friend.*

"I know this is only a costume," Grandma Bev said as her sewing machine hummed along. McKinley was at the smaller machine, working on the froofy sleeves. Once both pieces were finished, they'd attach them. "But I hate to leave the inside seams unfinished. It just feels sloppy."

"We could do a Hong Kong seam," McKinley suggested, remembering the technique Grandma Bev had taught her the day before she left.

"I don't think I know that one," Grandma Bev replied.

"Really?" McKinley was surprised. "But you . . ." She trailed off. "I could show you, maybe, if you want?"

At that, Grandma Bev smiled. "I'd love that."

McKinley beamed. She felt so lucky to be right here, in this moment.

Now if only she could get Billy to realize how lucky *he* was. Then she'd be one step closer to turning him into a better person—and making her own world better at the same time.

14

Mmm Mmm Mmm Mmm

McKinley and Grandma Bev were still hard at work when, an hour or so later, McKinley heard the familiar sound of the front door swinging open.

"Well, look who finally decided to drop in," Grandma Bev said as Billy scooted in through the door. Her tone was light, though, and she motioned for Billy to give her a hug—which, to McKinley's surprise, he did without fighting.

He did, however, give McKinley a death glare.

"I thought you would've left by now," he grumbled at her.

"Be civil, Billy," Grandma Bev replied. "Mickey and I have been hard at work while you were out doing whatever it is young hooligans do these days." McKinley noticed that Grandma Bev didn't ask Billy anything about where he'd been all this time or how he'd ended up on the Time Hop committee. If *she'd* stayed out past dark, her dad would've whipped out a megaphone to let the whole town know just how much trouble she was in. Instead, Grandma Bev held up the tablecloth dress to show her son. "We still need to hem it, but it looks incredible, don't you think? Your friend here is a real whiz."

Billy only rolled his eyes. Of course. Like he cared about McKinley or fashion.

But if Grandma Bev saw, she chose to ignore it. "Mickey, would you like to stay for dinner?" she asked.

And McKinley replied "Sure!" before she noticed the scowl on Billy's face. But whatever. It wasn't like she was going to pass up an opportunity to finally get to work crabbifying Billy. And if it gave her more time to spend with Grandma Bev, even better.

"Fabulous. Connie said she brought over a casserole, so you two can heat that up. Mickey, you're okay getting back to Jackie's by yourself?"

McKinley's head was spinning. "You're . . ." Grandma Bev was whipping a sweater over her shoulders. "You're leaving?"

"'Fraid so, doll. I am"—Grandma Bev looked at her watch—"oh dear, *very* late for class. Billy, do you have homework?" Billy shrugged at her. "Well, do it, would you? And don't stay up too late. You should be *ah-sleep* by the time I get home."

"Yeah, yeah," Billy said.

And just like that, Grandma Bev was out the door.

Billy lost no time turning on McKinley. "You can go now," he told her.

"I . . ." McKinley couldn't leave now. "Jackie and her dad already ate," she said. Which was probably true, anyway. "Just let me have dinner here, and then I'll go."

Billy let out an enormous sigh. "Fine," he said. "Whatever." He slumped off to the kitchen, and McKinley followed him. He whipped open the refrigerator door and buried his head inside. "There's no casserole in here," he said. He checked the freezer. Nothing.

McKinley frowned. "Yeah, I thought Aunt Connie said she was bringing it over tomorrow. Not today."

With one hand still on the open freezer door, Billy squinted an eye at her. "Why are you calling her *Aunt* Connie? She's not your aunt."

She's not yours either, McKinley wanted to say. But she knew what he meant. "That's . . . what your mom called her."

Apparently that explanation was enough for him, because Billy returned to examining the contents of the freezer. "Aha!" he cried suddenly. "Dinner!"

"You can't be serious," McKinley said, eyeing the carton of chocolate ice cream he pulled out. Who was this person, and what had he done with her father? "That's not, like, a *meal*."

Billy rolled his eyes again. "Feel free to eat whatever you want," he said, slapping the freezer door shut. "I'm having ice cream."

McKinley half wished she hadn't said anything. She never got to eat ice cream for dinner in her own time. But she couldn't exactly back down now. She opened the fridge to see what she was working with.

At McKinley's version of this house, the fridge was always stocked with healthy treats—berries, baby carrots, oat milk, salad fixings, you name it. Now there was only a crusty-topped bottle of mustard, a nearly empty container of cranberry juice (the super-sugary brand that McKinley's dad never let them buy), a carton of eggs, and some leftover Chinese food that—she flipped open the carton—was *way* past edible.

"What're you doing with those?" Billy asked, eyeing McKinley as she checked the expiration date on the eggs.

"Making scrambled eggs," she replied. She headed to the pantry and whipped open the door before realizing she probably should've asked where the spices were. She shuffled around some seriously ancient-looking canned veggies. The place was a *mess*. And there was no overhead light yet. But at last she found what she needed. Salt, pepper, garlic powder, olive oil, check. She whipped around and . . .

Smacked straight into Billy.

"Ack!" she cried, catching the spices before they tumbled to the ground. "What are you doing?"

"How do you know how to make scrambled eggs?" Billy asked. He seemed genuinely curious.

McKinley was surprised. "You don't?" After all, she'd learned it from him.

Billy seemed to think that snorting counted as an answer to McKinley's question. He headed to the cupboard for an ice-cream bowl.

He didn't stop watching her, though.

He watched as McKinley cracked the eggs, careful not to get any shell fragments inside the mixing bowl. He watched as she broke the yolks with a fork and whisked it all up. He watched as she added a little bit of salt, pepper, and garlic. And when the oil in the pan had heated up to a nice glistening shimmer, he watched as she dumped the whole lot inside with a sizzle. McKinley pretended she didn't notice him watching, but she did.

"That smells good," Billy said as the eggs began to cook. McKinley noticed he hadn't started scooping his ice cream yet.

"Want some?" she asked.

"No."

"Suit yourself." McKinley pushed the wet eggs around with the spatula, keeping a careful eye on them as they began to firm up. She only glanced at Billy out of the corner of her eye, but she was pretty sure he was still watching. He obviously wanted eggs. "Can I have some ice cream?" she asked him.

Billy thought about that. "I guess," he said slowly. "But only if you give me some eggs."

McKinley fought to keep the satisfied grin off her face. "Okay," she told him.

Billy grabbed a second bowl and spoon, along with two plates and two forks. Then he scooped out the ice cream while McKinley served up the eggs. Without a word, they moved to the dining room to sit down. And after clearing some space, they got to eating.

And now, McKinley thought, *it is time to get crabby.*

"You're pretty lucky, you know," she told Billy as she went to work on her eggs. They'd turned out pretty good, if she did say so herself. "Having a mom who lets you do whatever you want. I mean, no way I'd get away with coming home late or eating ice cream for dinner."

Billy didn't look up from his ice cream. "Mmm," he said.

"And Aunt—I mean, Connie—she seems pretty great, too. Always helping out, bringing you casseroles and stuff. And you have this great house, and this awesome town, and Ron—Ronny. He seems cool, right? So much stuff to be grateful for."

"Uh, okay, weirdo," Billy said through a mouthful of ice cream.

"You don't think your life is great?" she asked him.

Billy snorted. "Sure," he said. He kicked back the last of the cranberry juice, straight from the carton. "My life's perfect."

"I didn't say it was perfect," McKinley argued. "I know there's bad stuff, too. I'm just saying you have more good things in your life than you might think. So maybe you shouldn't act like such a jerk all the time."

"Mmm."

McKinley hated when he did that. He thought she didn't understand anything, but she *did*. "Okay, fine, I shouldn't've called you a jerk. I just meant that . . . everyone has problems."

"Like you know what my problems are."

"I know your dad died when you were really little," McKinley said. "And that's awful, obviously, but lots of people grow up with only one parent, and your mom is amazing."

The back of Billy's neck was beginning to flush red, but all he said was, "Mmm."

"And I know you have trouble in school," McKinley went on, "with bad grades and stuff, but that's only because of your—"

"I'm not stupid," Billy snapped at her.

McKinley blinked, startled. "I know," she told him.

"Who even are you?" Billy asked. "And why do you care so much if I like my life?"

"I just thought if you could, you know, appreciate the blessings in your life, it might help you be a better person."

"I think I'm pretty great the way I am, thanks," Billy told her. He had chocolate ice cream in the corners of his mouth that he was making no effort to wipe away.

McKinley found herself giving Billy a look that her dad liked to give her when she forgot her password to the online calendar. "Right," she said. "Because the kid who steals science projects and gets detention and bails out on helping people couldn't use *any* improving."

Billy growled into his bowl. "Who made you the boss of the universe?" he muttered.

"I'm not trying to boss you around," McKinley said. Her dad was missing the point as usual. "I just want to help."

"Why?"

McKinley opened her mouth, then closed it again. It was a fair question, but it wasn't like she could explain how she couldn't return to the future until she improved him. Finally she settled on half the truth. "Because I know things can be better," she said. "I know *you* can be better. And if I know how things *should* be, isn't it sort of my job to help you?"

"Mmm."

McKinley let out a long sigh. "Just promise me you'll think about it, okay? All the good things in your life, I mean," McKinley said. "Instead of only the bad stuff."

"Mmm."

Billy finished up the last of his ice cream and stared at his plate of eggs, the steam still rising off it. For a long moment, McKinley thought maybe he'd reject them altogether. But finally, he pulled the plate toward him and took a bite.

"Good?" McKinley asked about the eggs. Billy didn't answer. Not even an *mmm*. Still, he kept eating. McKinley moved on to her ice cream.

It was tasty.

They finished the rest of their makeshift dinner in silence.

McKinley was worried about saying anything else in case she ruined what little progress she might've made on the C.R.A.B.S. front. She just hoped that Billy actually took her advice about counting his blessings.

As she was bringing her dishes to the kitchen sink, the phone rang. Billy answered it.

"It's for you!" he hollered, and when McKinley made it back out to the living room, he was holding out the phone on its long green cord like it was a hairy spider he'd rather not have anywhere near him. McKinley grabbed it.

"Uh, hello?" she said.

"Hey," Jackie replied from the other end. She was whispering like she thought she was in some sort of spy movie. "You have to come back. I dug something up, and it's *huge*. This could change everything."

And before McKinley could say anything, Jackie hung up.

"What'd *she* want?" Billy asked.

McKinley stared at the receiver. It was letting out a monotone buzz in her hand. "How do you hang this thing up?" she asked. "There's no buttons on it."

Billy snatched the receiver out of her hand. When he set it back on the cradle, the buzzing stopped. "When did you say you were going back to wherever you came from?" he asked her.

McKinley cleared her throat. "Soon," she said, hoping that was truer than not.

Then she scooped her backpack off the floor and headed out the door to find out what it was that Jackie had discovered.

15

What's Up?

When McKinley stepped into Jackie's bedroom ten minutes later, Jackie didn't even bother to say hello. She just thrust a piece of paper at McKinley and declared, "The plot thickens!"

"What's this?" McKinley asked, turning the paper right-side up. It was blurry, and the words were tiny.

"It's a printout from the microfiche machine," Jackie explained.

Man, McKinley missed the internet.

"I stayed late at the library to try to find stuff about Billy," Jackie continued, "but Mr. Deisler kept peeking over my shoulder to make sure I was 'on task.'" She plopped herself down on her bed and rooted through the drawer of her side table, finally pulling out a pack of Twizzlers. "I still can't believe there are going to be grape-flavored Twizzlers one day," she said as she ripped open the package. She yanked off a bite with her teeth. "The future sounds magical."

"Jackie!" McKinley shook the paper at her. "Focus! Why'd you give me this weird article?" The headline read *One-Year Anniversary of "Gobbler Moon Man" Incident.*

"Oh, yeah, so"—Jackie paused to unstick some Twizzler from

her tooth—"I had to look up stuff from 1939, just so Mr. Deisler would get off my back. I wasn't even thinking there'd be anything that could help us, but then—*wham!*" She nodded at the printout. "Go ahead, read it."

While Jackie chewed, McKinley read. And with each word, McKinley became more and more convinced that spending too much time in the library must be bad for your brain. Because there was nothing in the article that seemed even remotely useful.

One-Year Anniversary of "Gobbler Moon Man" Incident

June 6, 1939
Gap Bend, PA

Today marks one year since a mysterious young man calling himself "Rufus" caused a commotion at the Gobbler Diner. Dressed in clothing that could only be cataloged as "curious," the youth spoke spiritedly of moon landings and other shocking subjects, such as bass-playing beetles and lamps made of lava. Patrons soon surmised that this vexing visitor must be a spaceman—who else, they concluded, would mutter such marvels? While many were delighted by the diversion, others were not. Mrs. Belinda Dalloworth (who, as readers well know, has a famously feeble frame) fainted straight from her chair. Constable Nolan was alerted to attend to her, but before he arrived, the funny fellow had fled the scene. Fortunately, budding photographer Hogarth Watson snapped this striking shot before the outsider slipped outside, never to be spotted again.

Readers will be relieved to learn that Mrs. Dalloworth insists she incurred no injury from the episode. Instead, she believes the sinister skirmish produced in her a preternatural proclivity for preparing popovers. Inquisitive individuals may buy Belinda's baked goods at the annual Jelly Jamboree in July.

McKinley plopped down in Jackie's desk chair, skimming the article again. "I don't get it," she said. "What's a popover?"

"No," Jackie said. "That's not the . . . Don't you see?" She ripped off another chunk of Twizzler and chewed while she spoke. "Moon landings? Lava lamps? The Beatles? That guy they're talking about, he wasn't a 'spaceman.' He *time traveled*, just like you."

"You really think so?" McKinley squinted harder at the page, like that might help her figure out the truth.

"It's perfect timing, too," Jackie went on. "Because usually in stories, when the main character starts to, like, *really* struggle, they usually meet someone who gives them some answers. Like when Wilbur meets Charlotte in *Charlotte's Web*. Or when Obi-Wan takes Luke under his wing in *Star Wars*." She waved her half-gnawed candy around to emphasize her point. McKinley was beginning to wonder if grown-up Jackie conducted editorial meetings with her mouth full of candy. "So now it's time for *you* to meet *your* wise, older mentor."

McKinley thought about that. "Even if you're right about this guy," she said, "we don't have any idea who he—"

Jackie tapped the newspaper photo with the end of her

Twizzler. "Who do we know," she said slowly, clearly enjoying the moment, "named *Rufus*?"

McKinley brought the paper close to her nose. The teenager in the photo had a buzz-cut hairdo, bell-bottom jeans, and a black turtleneck. He definitely looked out of place with all the men in roomy suit jackets and women in collared floral dresses. But he *did* look a little like . . .

"Mr. *Jones*?" McKinley squeaked.

When McKinley looked up, Jackie was already holding the receiver of her neon-pink phone. It was doing that weird buzzing thing.

"There's only one way to find out," Jackie replied with a grin.

McKinley almost hoped no one would answer the phone, but after only three rings, she heard her teacher's familiar snarl.

"Who is this?"

"Um . . ." McKinley glanced at Jackie, who gave her an encouraging thumbs-up from across the bed. "I'm, um, Mickey Wells? From school? I broke the head off Gregory Groundhog?"

"How did you get this number? Why are you calling? It's after eight p.m., child. Haven't your parents taught you any manners?" The surly questions came shooting out rapid fire. "I'm giving you detention, Wells, first thing tomorrow."

"You already . . ." McKinley locked eyes with Jackie, who was giving her serious *Spit it out* vibes. McKinley took a deep breath. What did she have to lose, anyway? "I know you time traveled," she said. "When you were a teenager." And before Mr. Jones could argue, she added, "I time traveled, too, from 2018. And I need your help to get back."

There was a long silence on the other end of the phone, and McKinley started to worry that Mr. Jones had fainted right from his chair, like famously feeble Belinda Dalloworth. "Are you okay?"

"Meet me at the Gobbler Diner in fifteen minutes," Mr. Jones replied. "Don't tell *anyone* where you're going." Then he hung up. There was nothing in McKinley's ear but a low buzz.

16

Mr. Jones

Even though he was the one who'd invited her, Mr. Jones looked anything but thrilled to see McKinley when she and Jackie slid into the vinyl booth across from him.

"I said not to tell anyone," he growled.

It was a dark night, with very little moon to speak of. The diner was nearly empty, just one family with grown kids eating pie, and a few lone customers scattered here and there, reading newspapers and sipping coffee. Out the window, cars drove by lazily, like even they were getting ready for bed.

"She was sitting right next to me when you said that," McKinley told him. "She heard the whole thing."

"Plus," Jackie added, "I was the one who figured it out." She slid the printout across the table.

Mr. Jones frowned at the article but didn't pick it up. He wrapped his hands around a mug of tea and glared at McKinley. "How do I know you're telling the truth about where you came from?" he asked, his voice low.

McKinley took a deep breath, thinking. She could tell him all about Snapchat and *Fortnite*, but she had the feeling those weren't the sorts of things that would convince Mr. Jones. Instead, her mind wandered back to what Jackie had said when McKinley had shown up on her doorstep. "Well," McKinley reasoned, "wouldn't it be a super-weird thing to lie about?"

Mr. Jones harrumphed at that. But he didn't argue either.

"McKinley, er, *Mickey*," Jackie said, "zoomed back in time when she was at the Time Hop. They were celebrating 1993, and then *boom!* She was here for real."

Mr. Jones took a slow sip of tea. Then another. McKinley folded and unfolded the napkin in front of her, waiting for him to say something.

And then, at last, he spoke.

"I can hide you in my garage," he said. "It's not too cold at night right now, and I haven't seen any raccoons in a while, so you should be fine."

"Um . . ." McKinley wasn't sure what the normal response was when someone told you they'd time traveled, but she was pretty sure that wasn't it. "No," she said. "I don't . . . We just wanted to know how you got back to your own time. What did you have to change before you were sent back? Was it a person? We think the person I'm supposed to change is—"

"No!" Mr. Jones slapped the table so hard his tea sloshed out of his mug. A few folks at nearby tables looked over to see what the fuss was, but Mr. Jones glared them into turning back. Then he leaned across the table to speak more quietly to the girls. "Don't you understand?" he hissed. "You can't change *anything*." He snatched the napkin McKinley held out to him and began mopping up his tea without any sort of thanks. "I was lucky to get back to my own timeline without making any ripples. If this second glitch causes so much as a—"

"What d'ya mean, 'glitch'?" Jackie asked. And then, before he could answer, she stopped a passing waitress and told her, "I'll take a slice of chocolate cake and a strawberry milkshake, please. Oh, and ice cream on the side, thanks. He's paying." She jerked her chin at Mr. Jones, who looked stampeding-rhinoceros mad. "Mickey, you want anything?"

McKinley shook her head. Was there any situation where Jackie *didn't* want junk food? "I'm good," she replied.

"I'm not paying for that," Mr. Jones said as the waitress headed off to place the order.

"You're the one who invited us here," Jackie argued. "So it should be your treat. That's only polite."

"I didn't—"

McKinley thought maybe she should intervene before the vein in Mr. Jones's forehead got huge enough to become an Instagram influencer. "You were saying?" she reminded him. "About a glitch?"

He took a short sip of his tea, as though to calm himself. But he was still making furious squint eyes at Jackie.

"You can call it whatever you want," Mr. Jones told them. "Glitch. Anomaly. Error. I don't know how it happened—maybe time folded in on itself for a second, maybe it skipped like a record. But however I was sent back that day, I wasn't supposed to be. Just like you aren't supposed to be here now."

"How do you know it's a mistake?" McKinley asked.

"Yeah," Jackie piped up. "How do you know the universe didn't pick you guys to go back in time and do something specific?"

"Because history is *history*!" Mr. Jones pounded on the table again, but there was too little of his tea left to slosh out this time. "The events that unfolded aren't mine to change, or yours, or anyone else's."

McKinley wrinkled her nose. She hated to argue with her own history teacher, but . . . "You went back to 1938, right?" Mr. Jones nodded. "Wasn't that, like, *right* before World War II started?" She remembered the date because of Mr. Jones's history class, but she didn't want to give him the satisfaction of knowing that. "So why didn't you say anything about it? You could've saved all those people. Stopped the atom bomb from being dropped." Honestly, you'd think a history teacher would've thought of that. "But instead you just did . . . nothing?"

"I didn't do *nothing*," Mr. Jones replied. That forehead vein was so big, it would have been up to five million followers now, easy. "I made sure not to step on any butterflies."

"Um, what?" McKinley said.

That's when the waitress came back with Jackie's order. The three of them leaned back to make room for all the desserts.

"Enjoy!" the waitress told them before scurrying off.

"It's like that Ray Bradbury story," Jackie said. She was already deep into her cake. "'A Sound of Thunder.' This guy goes back in time to see dinosaurs"—she paused for a loud slurp of her milkshake—"only he accidentally steps on a butterfly while he's there. And when he gets back to his own time, the world's, like, *totally* different." She glanced up at their teacher. "Is that what you meant?"

"More or less," Mr. Jones grumbled.

Jackie pumped a fist in the air. "Woohoo, A-plus for Jackie!" she shouted.

Mr. Jones was not amused. "The point is," he went on, "we have no idea how one blip on the timeline affects anything else. Even a tiny event, something seemingly inconsequential, could lead to bigger and bigger changes, ultimately ending in catastrophe."

"Still . . ." McKinley began. "World War II seems like a safe thing to try to change."

He shot her a look like she'd just bombed a test, hard. "Any single thing you say or do," he told her sternly, "could create a new history that's even worse. Does that seem like a safe thing to gamble on?"

"To be fair," Jackie chimed in, wiping her mouth with her sweatshirt sleeve, "a teenager shouting about bombs and Hitler probably wasn't going to do much, anyway. Even the people he met here"—she waved her arms around the diner—"thought he was completely nuts."

"Yeah . . ." McKinley couldn't really argue with that. It wasn't like she could storm the White House right now and insist that President Clinton pay more attention to global warming. Jackie's point made her realize something else, though. "But you *did* step on butterflies," she told Mr. Jones. She pointed to the article half-hidden under Jackie's bowl of ice cream. "All those people, they saw you. You told them tons of stuff about the future."

Mr. Jones pinched the bridge of his nose. "That was a huge mistake," he said. "Never should've happened." He brought his mug to his lips but didn't drink any tea, just held it there for a moment before speaking again.

McKinley waited patiently.

Jackie slurped her milkshake.

"When the glitch happened," he went on at last, "it was 1969 in my time, the evening before *Apollo 11* was scheduled to land on the moon. I didn't even want to be at the Time Hop that night, but my parents insisted I join them because I'd been spending all day glued to the television, terrified something would go wrong with the mission. I knew even the tiniest slipup could ruin everything, and I couldn't bear the chance that those astronauts—our country, humanity—could be *this close* to making history, only to watch it slip away." He took a slow sip of tea, then set his mug back down. "I know it seems unremarkable to you kids now, that man has walked on the moon, but back then, no one knew if it could or would be done. If either of you ever has the good fortune to live through an unprecedented human achievement—you'll understand how I was feeling."

"I get it," McKinley said. "Like when *Pokémon GO* came out a few years ago, and it was *so* epic that Meg's cousin Wallace actually ran his bike into a tree trying to nab a Mewtwo."

"Stop!" Mr. Jones said, stuffing his hands over his ears like a two-year-old. "Haven't you been listening? If you tell anyone *anything* about what hasn't happened yet, you risk altering the entire course of human history."

McKinley wasn't so sure about that. "I might alter the course of human history by telling you about *Pokémon GO*?" she asked.

"The point is," Mr. Jones growled at her, "you don't *know* what will alter it. That's why, when the glitch happened to me, I hid myself away—after I figured out what was going on." He shook his head. "I'm sorry to say it took me a few hours to process everything. After I left the school, I saw lots of people in unusual clothes, but I figured they'd come from the Time Hop, too—the theme was 1938 that year. So when I got here, to the Gobbler, it didn't occur to me that I shouldn't ask about the moon landing. But, as you read"—he shot eye-daggers at the article—"*that* blew up completely. As soon as I pieced together what had happened, I made sure not to interact with another soul. I slept in a tree in Buckle Park. I snuck food out of trash cans. Because I couldn't risk something I said or did jeopardizing those astronauts or anything else. It was my duty to protect history."

"And when you got back—to your own time, I mean"— McKinley scratched her nose—"was anything different than before you left?"

"Nothing." At this, Mr. Jones finally allowed himself a smile. It looked uncomfortable with the rest of his face. "That's how I knew I'd been successful. Everything was exactly how I'd left it."

While McKinley mulled that over, Jackie scooched her ice-cream bowl toward herself with a loud *screech!* across the table. "Where were you when you first went back in time?" she asked. "Was it the girls' bathroom, like McKinley? No judgment."

Mr. Jones let out an exasperated breath. McKinley had the feeling he must make that noise a lot, teaching Jackie. "I don't know when it happened, precisely. Early afternoon, perhaps? Like I said, it took me some time to understand what was going on. But I can assure you I was *not* in the girls' bathroom."

Mr. Jones might not have been as cool a "wise, older mentor" as Charlotte the spider or Obi-Wan Kenobi, McKinley thought, but he did know some stuff that could be helpful, at least.

"What about when you returned to your own time?" McKinley asked. "How did that work? What did you have to do?"

Cue the third table slap of the evening.

"I didn't *do* anything!" Mr. Jones cried. "That's the whole point! I just . . . came back." He scratched at the skin of his thumb, like he was remembering. "I spent a handful of days in 1938, and then, suddenly, I was back where I started. No rhyme or reason for it, except that it was the Time Hop that day, too, in 1938, the same as it was when I first traveled. For whatever reason, the glitch seems to be tied to that event."

"Oh, *good*," McKinley said. So she wouldn't be stuck in the '90s forever. She'd get to go home to Meg again and Grandma Bev. Her bed. Her phone. McKinley rolled her shoulders, working out a little of the stress she hadn't realized she'd been holding on to. "The Time Hop's just . . ." She did the math in her head. "One more week? Tomorrow's Saturday, right? I can do that."

"Of course you can," Mr. Jones agreed. "I'll make space in my garage as soon as we leave here."

"No way," Jackie said, licking the back of her ice-cream spoon. "Sorry, Mr. J. You are *not* hiding my friend in your garage for a week and feeding her dumpster food."

Mr. Jones frowned. "It's a *converted* garage," he said, like that was the issue. "With a foldout bed. I'm not a monster."

"She's just fine at my house, thanks," Jackie replied.

"Young lady, I don't think you understand the gravity of—"

But for once, McKinley felt as confident as Jackie.

"No," she said. Firmly. "Jackie's right. I'm not going to do that, Mr. Jones."

"*Young. Lady,*" he growled. "You—"

"I've already been to school," McKinley replied. "So if I just vanish into thin air, don't you think *that* will cause more of a fuss than anything? What if someone realizes I'm hanging out with your garage raccoons? You think it would alter history if all your students thought you kidnapped one of their classmates?"

Mr. Jones opened his mouth to argue. But he couldn't. McKinley was right, and he knew it.

McKinley nodded, one short nod. "So"—she made to stand up—"I'll see you on Monday."

"Not so fast," Mr. Jones told her.

McKinley plopped back down.

"You are a history keeper now," he said, and he pointed his finger at her as he spoke. "You have a job, an important one. Your interactions with other people must be short, limited. You may tell no one *anything* about the future, even if you think it will help them. You may make no attempt to change anything. Your conversations with your fellow students will be brief and meaningless. When you're not in class, you'll be at Jackie's house. Nowhere else. As of this minute, I'm pulling you from the Time Hop committee."

"But—" Sewing costumes with Grandma Bev was one of the few things McKinley had truly been enjoying about time travel.

"If I get wind you're not following my rules," Mr. Jones said, cutting her off, "I'll make trouble for you, and fast."

And McKinley believed him. She shut her mouth.

Mr. Jones picked up his mug then, and he looked hard at both girls before he said what he did next.

"The universe may have made a mistake throwing you backward in time," he told them, "but *we* won't." Then he tipped back the mug to take a long glug, even though the last of his tea was gone.

17

Linger

It wasn't a far walk from the Gobbler back to Jackie's house—nothing was a far walk in Gap Bend. But that night it seemed to McKinley that time was twisting up like a pretzel all over again, making five-block walks feel eons long. The air was thick with near-summer humidity, the sky was dark, and McKinley had a lot to think about.

"I can't believe the universe picked *that* guy to time travel," Jackie said. "I could name like fifty people who'd be better time travelers than Mr. Jones!"

McKinley heard a soft rattling and glanced over to discover that Jackie had ripped open a box of Nerds.

"I always keep candy in my pocket for emergencies," Jackie explained, pouring out a handful. She offered some to McKinley.

"Thanks," McKinley said, and she popped a few in her mouth. "So you think Mr. Jones was wrong about it being a glitch?" she asked.

Jackie snorted. "You really think the universe can *mess up?*"

McKinley crunched her candy without responding. The truth was, she had no idea.

"Mr. Jones is thinking like a history teacher," Jackie went on. "Like there's all this stuff that's *supposed* to happen, and you can't—you shouldn't—change it, no matter what." She paused for another mouthful of Nerds. "But if you think about it like a *writer*, then you see life is more like a story. And in a story, the characters are *supposed* to grow and change and make things around them change, too."

McKinley frowned. "But Mr. Jones didn't change anything," she argued. "He said that when he got back to his own time, everything was exactly the same as before he left."

"Exactly," Jackie replied. "Because he's the worst main character ever written. Totally flat." She rattled the box of Nerds as they crossed Flume Street. "Think about it. If Mr. Jones *had* changed stuff when he time traveled, then when he got back to the future, his life would've been way better, and that would've made *him* better, too. And if he wasn't such a miserable grump all the time, I bet he wouldn't stink so much as a teacher. Not, like, yelling and snarling all the time?" McKinley had to agree that she'd definitely prefer to sit through fifth-period World History with this pretend version of Mr. Jones than the real one. "Just imagine all the students he could've inspired, and all the great things they might've done. Like fixed cancer or figured out a way to stop Butterfingers from sticking to the bottom of your teeth." McKinley nodded. The idea was intriguing, at least. "Only all that great stuff?" Jackie went on. "It never happened. All because Mr. Jones was too freaked out to leave the dumpster."

McKinley felt like her brain was attempting to doggy-paddle through Jell-O. "I do like the idea of being in charge of my own story . . ." she said slowly.

"Of course you do," Jackie said. "Who wouldn't? So you get back to work changing your dad, and I'll make sure I marry *anyone* but Ronny, and by the time you're whisked home at the Time Hop next week, both our futures will be totally perfect."

That's when McKinley began choking on her Nerds. "Wait, *what*?" she coughed, pounding on her chest. "You don't want to marry Ron anymore?"

"He's *Little Ronny Rothstein*," Jackie replied, like that was enough of an explanation. "He eats his own toenails."

McKinley coughed again. "He does not." *Cough, cough.*

Jackie tilted her head back to empty the Nerds box into her mouth. "He might," she said. "Anyway, now that you've warned me I was *going* to marry him, I can make sure I *don't*. So"—she crunched a loud crunch—"thanks."

"But . . ." McKinley wasn't wading through Jell-O anymore. She was drowning. "If you don't marry Ron, then Meg will never be born."

Jackie crushed the empty box and stuck it in the back pocket of her shorts. "I'll marry someone else," she said. "Someone less . . . *Ronny*. And I'll have kids with that guy."

"But they won't be *Meg*," McKinley argued. "She's your daughter. How can you not want to have your own daughter?"

"Whichever kids I have *will* be my kids," Jackie said. "And you can be best friends with them."

"No!" McKinley said. Jell-O in her lungs. Jell-O everywhere. "Jackie, you can't do that." McKinley couldn't imagine going back to her own time only to find that Meg no longer existed.

"She *has* to be there. She's . . . *Meg*. And . . ." McKinley had to stop walking just to get the words out. "I can't let the last thing that happened be . . ." *Why* had McKinley gotten in that dumb fight with Meg and said what she said? "I didn't even *olive loaf*," she moaned.

"Huh?"

McKinley took a deep, calming breath. *In. Out. In. Out.* She had to find a way to make Jackie understand. "We got in a fight," she said slowly. "At the Time Hop, right before I came here. And I should've . . . There's this thing we always say to each other." *In. Out. In. Out.* "'Olive loaf.' It's our secret friend code that we've been doing forever because when you mouth it without any sound it looks like you're saying—"

"'I love you,'" Jackie said, cutting her off.

McKinley squinted at her friend in the dark. "How'd you know that?"

"My mom used to say it to me," Jackie replied, "before she died." She scratched her cheek. "I guess in the future I must say it to Meg. Maybe that's where you guys get it from."

McKinley allowed herself a smile. "Yeah," she said. "I bet it is." *In. Out.* "See? You must love Meg a lot if you taught her that. So you know how important she is. And I can't just let her disappear without getting a chance to tell her I know it, too."

It was Jackie's turn to take a deep breath then. *In. Out.* Then another.

In.

Out.

McKinley waited.

In.

Out.

"I just think," Jackie said at last, "that if you get to change things about your life, then I should get to, too. And I know it's not what you'd decide, but . . ." She shrugged her shoulders. "Don't you think it should be up to me who I marry?"

McKinley felt a pit in her stomach like nothing she'd ever felt before. *No*, she wanted to say. *Not if you're choosing wrong.* But before she could find the words that would change Jackie's mind for good, Jackie was off walking down the sidewalk again.

"You coming?" Jackie asked when she realized McKinley hadn't joined her.

"Yeah," McKinley said. "Yeah, of course." But no matter how hard she tried to shake it, there was that worry, deep in her gut, that simply wouldn't go away.

18

Ice Cream

"Y ou have to come out sometime, you know," Jackie said, walking into the bedroom Sunday morning.

"*Snrfblz*," McKinley replied. It was the sound, apparently, that one made after thirty-seven hours zipped inside a sleeping bag. She'd hidden herself away in there ever since they'd gotten home from the Gobbler, only emerging for occasional potty breaks. Now McKinley popped her head out, tucking the edge of the sleeping bag under her chin. "I'm fine right here," she told Jackie. "I've got plenty to eat"—she gestured to the open drawer of Jackie's nightstand, which was mostly empty candy-bar wrappers— "and all the entertainment I need, thank you." She tugged out Jackie's copy of *Latawnya, the Naughty Horse, Learns to Say "No" to Drugs.* "Honestly, it's like a vacation in here. Who needs sunlight?"

Her teeth tasted like moss.

Jackie flopped onto the bed, stomach down, hands under her chin. "I know you're freaked out," she said, "but I promise you're not going to rip apart the fabric of time if you leave the house." She stretched out her hand to rustle through her candy stash. "Tell me you didn't eat all the Chewy SweeTARTS."

McKinley pulled the half-empty package from the depths of the sleeping bag.

"Thanks," Jackie said, quickly stuffing two pieces into her mouth whole.

McKinley stared at Jackie's ceiling. "What if Mr. Jones was right about not changing anything, though?" she said, her voice flat. "Maybe I should just stay here until the Time Hop,"

Jackie raised a skeptical eyebrow. "If you're starting to agree with that guy," she said, "then you *definitely* need to get out of there. You were obviously sent back in time for a reason. And it wasn't to lie around smelling up my bedroom."

"I don't smell," McKinley argued. She'd messed everything up already just by being here. A world without Meg was not one she wanted to live in. The only thing to do now was to stay huddled in a ball forever and pray she didn't somehow make things even worse.

Jackie sighed. "Look. While you were eating all my candy yesterday, I did some more research. And there's something I need to show you. But you need to leave the sleeping bag to see it."

"But—"

"We won't talk to anyone," Jackie said, hands up like she was swearing an oath. "This will be an observation mission only."

McKinley took her deep, calming breaths. *In, out. In, out.*

"Okay," she said slowly. "If you promise I don't have to interact with anyone."

"Scout's honor."

And even though she wasn't 100 percent sure it was the right thing to do, McKinley unzipped herself from the sleeping bag.

"But, um, maybe before we leave," Jackie began slowly, "you might want to . . . shower?"

McKinley threw a pillow at her.

And then she headed to the bathroom. Because Jackie was right about one thing, at least.

McKinley smelled *rank*.

"I feel like this is defeating the purpose of the whole showering thing," McKinley told Jackie. She didn't know where she'd expected Jackie to take her that morning, but it sure wasn't a step aerobics class. At the moment, she and Jackie were hopping up and down on plastic step platforms to the song "Rhythm Is a Dancer" with about a dozen women dressed in neon biker pants and patterned leotards. "You planning on telling me why we're here yet?"

After a pause for a complicated *turn-kick-clap-step-up-down!* Jackie said, "Okay, see that woman up there?" Fortunately, the music was loud enough that they didn't have to worry too much about being overheard. "With the short blond hair?"

"What about her?" McKinley asked. *Right-kick-left-kick!* From the back row, it was hard to see the instructor, and McKinley was terrified that if she messed up the choreography, she might trip over her platform and give the lady in front of her a concussion. And what if that lady was supposed to become a nuclear physicist or something? So even though the song blasting through the room was telling her to "lift your hands and voices, free your mind and join us," McKinley was finding that kind of tough when the entire course of human history was one wrong dance move away from total destruction.

"Her name's Denise Ferriden," Jackie replied. *And-kick-and-step-and-down-and-clap!*

McKinley studied the woman's reflection in the mirror. "I know her," she said. "From Ferriden Electric." This Denise looked much younger than the fiftysomething version McKinley was familiar with, but that was Gap Bend's number one electrician all right. Last year Denise had painted an awesome new logo across the back of her van: KEEPING GAP BEND LIT! *Clap-and-kick-up-down-and-kick!* "What about her?"

That's when Jackie *step-toe-step-CRASH!*ed herself into the side wall with a bang loud enough to disrupt the "boxerobics" class next door.

"How about a water break?" McKinley suggested, offering her friend a hand up. She figured maybe she wasn't the only one who should be worried about hospitalizing physicists.

"Good idea," Jackie muttered, rubbing her backside.

As they sipped from paper cups at the watercooler near the door, Jackie dug through her backpack. "Aha!" she cried, and she tugged out a book. *A History of Gap Bend: Revised and Updated.* Jackie turned to a page marked with a purple Post-it and pointed to a grainy black-and-white picture. "Who does that look like to you?" she asked McKinley.

In the photo, a small blond-haired white girl with a huge smile was being hoisted into the air by two men in old-fashioned work jumpsuits. The caption read *The hero of the Great Gap Bend Blackout of 1947, ten-year-old Denise, who was able to access a crawl space none of the town's electricians could squeeze through, enjoys an "energetic" celebration.*

As inconspicuously as she could, McKinley compared the girl in the photo with Denise's reflection in the mirror. (*Step-hop-twist!* went the class.) "I guess they do look a little alike," she admitted.

Jackie tossed her soggy paper cup in the wastebasket. "I bet you a million bucks that's the same person," she said. "And it proves that Mr. Jones is wrong, too, because Denise changed plenty while she was back there. The book says none of the town's electricians could fit into the space they needed to access to get power back to the town, so Denise volunteered to crawl through it. And nothing, like, *exploded* because she did that. It says the mayor was so happy he gave her a bucket of licorice wheels as thanks." Jackie took the book back. "I wish the mayor would thank me with buckets of candy."

"But you can't be *positive* that's her," McKinley said, squinting at Denise in the mirror again.

Jackie zipped up her backpack. "I figured you'd say that," she replied. And she tugged on McKinley's arm. "Come on. We've had enough exercise for one day."

The next stop on their *What the heck's your point, Jackie?* tour was Huckle Buck's Ice-Cream Parlor. While Jackie bought them cones, McKinley did her best to blend into the scenery. The space hadn't changed much in twenty-five years. It still had that old-timey vibe going for it, with small marble tables and chairs with curlicue designs crafted from iron.

"One scoop of Huckle Buckle Berry Bliss for you," Jackie

announced, sliding into the seat across from McKinley. "And one for me."

As McKinley licked the drips that were already slinking their way down the side of the cone, she decided to officially forgive Jackie for dragging her out of her sleeping bag. After the Time Hop, Huckle Buckle Berry Bliss ice cream was the second-most fabulous thing about Gap Bend. "Not that I'm complaining," McKinley said, taking another lick, "but why are we here?"

Jackie had already snarfed down nearly half her cone. "The girl with the braids," she said, darting her eyes to the counter. Her voice was low, but it probably didn't matter much—the trio of toddlers at the next table over were making more noise than a wood-chipper truck after Christmas.

McKinley followed Jackie's gaze to the teenage ice-cream scooper behind the counter. Just like her coworkers, the girl was wearing a blue-and-white-striped shirt with a rounded collar and black slacks. She stood out, though, for her two long brown braids, one hanging over each shoulder. "She doesn't look familiar," McKinley said.

"She's a sophomore at GBPS," Jackie told her. "Shannon Montague."

"Oh, I do know her," McKinley said. Jackie was fumbling through her backpack while simultaneously devouring her ice cream, and it was bound to end in disaster. "I think she's the head chef at this fancy new restaurant in town. I've never been, obviously, because veering from my dad's dinner schedule is, like, a crime worse than murder." McKinley rolled her eyes. "But you told me about it, actually, after you went there for your anniversary with . . ." McKinley trailed off. Best not to mention Jackie's future husband again if she didn't have to. "And, um, you said it was amazing."

Jackie nodded, plopping her book on the table. It was opened to a chapter entitled "A New Flavor Makes History."

"This whole chapter is about the Huckle Buck," Jackie explained. "According to this"—she skimmed her finger down the page—"in 1909, the old soda shop was losing business, so they decided to have an ice-cream-flavor contest to drum up publicity. And guess what the winning flavor was?"

McKinley snapped off the top edge of her cone with her teeth. "Huckle Buckle Berry Bliss," she said as she crunched. "You didn't need a book for that, you know." She pointed to the wall beside the counter, where the Huckle Buck's origin story was painted in cursive, along with drawings of tall crystal ice-cream goblets and juicy blue huckleberries.

"True," Jackie replied. "But the wall doesn't say *this* part." She read out loud. "'The suggestion for the flavor came from a child, an out-of-towner, who curiously refused to share her name—or even stick around long enough to taste her winning concoction. For months, in fact, townspeople attempted to locate the shy girl with the long brown braids and star-shaped mole, but she seemed to have vanished just as mysteriously as she'd arrived.'"

By the time Jackie slapped the book shut, McKinley was too busy staring at the front counter to care about the trail of Huckle Buckle Berry Bliss snaking its way down her arm.

Shannon had a mole shaped like a star, just under her left eye.

McKinley turned to Jackie and took a breath. "But if you're wrong, though . . ." she started.

Jackie handed McKinley a napkin for her arm. "We've got one more stop," she said, popping the tip of her ice-cream cone into her mouth. "If this doesn't convince you, nothing will." Then she pointed to McKinley's ice cream. "You gonna finish that or what?"

19

Explain It to Me

The ticket line outside the Gap Bend Cineplex was moving more slowly than one of those dial-up internet connections. It had started to rain on their walk over, and now McKinley was crammed up against the dozen or so other people in line, all trying to escape the drizzle underneath the one narrow awning. In McKinley's time there were touch screen machines inside the lobby.

McKinley checked out the NOW PLAYING poster on the wall beside them. "Are you sure we need to watch the *Super Mario Bros.* movie for you to prove whatever point you're trying to make?" she asked Jackie. "'Cause it looks kind of terrible."

Jackie shrugged. "If there's popcorn involved, who cares if the movie's bad? Anyway, it's not my fault this is what's playing. If you'd crash-landed here one week later, we could be seeing that one." She pointed to the *Jurassic Park* poster, which read COMING FRIDAY! McKinley was immediately reminded of the Time Hop and the dinosaur sculptures, and her fight with Meg, and everything. "Blame the universe, not me."

McKinley kicked at a piece of gravel that had made its way outside a decorative planter, trying to kick away her thoughts along with it. Like a person could just forget that they may have completely erased the existence of their very best friend.

"You ready to get down to business?" Jackie asked, yanking her book out of her backpack again.

McKinley wasn't so sure she was. "Let me guess," she replied. She checked to make sure no one could hear them, but they were the last people in line, and the guy in front of them was listening to one of those CD-player things with foam-covered headphones. "That dog over there"—she pointed to a man walking his cocker spaniel—"traveled to the 1600s, and when he came back he starred in the all-dog version of *Romeo and Juliet*."

"Wait, is that a real movie?" Jackie asked. "Because that sounds pretty sweet."

McKinley laughed so hard she had to swipe at her nose to check that she hadn't snorted out anything disgusting. "I was joking!" she said. "But, yeah, I would watch that, too."

"If you were a different sort of person," Jackie said thoughtfully, "you could really mess with me, you know? Like, 'In the future, everyone has their own jet pack, and cars can drive themselves, and the president gets paid in marshmallows.'"

"One of those is actually true," McKinley told her.

"Is it the marshmallow one?" Jackie asked, excited.

McKinley laughed again. "No."

"Guess I'm never running for president, then."

Jackie opened up the book. But she didn't flip any pages. She just sort of stared at the title page for a moment, until finally, without looking up, she said, "I'm really glad you crash-landed into my timeline, you know. It's been kind of cool having you around. I don't . . ." She shuffled her feet, like she wasn't quite sure what to say. Or maybe she just needed an extra breath to say it. "I don't always have that many people to hang out with."

"Oh." McKinley was surprised by that. Although now that she thought about it, McKinley hadn't actually seen Jackie with any other friends since she'd arrived. "It's been cool getting to hang out with you, too," she said. "I mean, the non-mom version of you." And she bumped Jackie's shoulder a little to make sure the words sunk in.

But maybe McKinley bumped a little *too* hard, because suddenly she had a weird feeling in her chest, like she was friend-cheating on Meg. She cleared her throat. "All right. Why are we here, for real?"

Jackie gestured with her elbow to the man behind the ticket booth. "You know Miguel?" she asked.

"Sure." Even decades younger, Miguel Rosas was instantly recognizable. His was one of the few Mexican American families in Gap Bend, for one thing, and his long hair was pulled back into exactly the same low ponytail that he always wore in 2018. "He owns the theater," McKinley said. "He's really nice. Sometimes he'll even give me free Jujubes, 'cause he says me and him are the only people in town who truly appreciate them."

Jackie wrinkled her nose up on her face. "Oh, McKinley, there are *such* better candies." She sounded severely disappointed, like a parent whose child had dropped their phone in the bathtub.

"Weren't you trying to tell me something important?" McKinley reminded her.

"Right. Okay." Jackie focused on the book again. "So this part is all about the Cineplex and how Miguel and his dad bought it when he was just nineteen. Apparently it was super run-down and set to be demolished, but at the very last minute, Miguel decided they should rescue it and restore it. That was just a couple years back, actually. It was a really big deal because for a while there, we had to drive all the way to Philly just to see a movie."

"Whoa, really?" In McKinley's time, the Cineplex was famous for its charity events and film screenings. It was nearly impossible to imagine Gap Bend without it. "Okay, so then what's your theo—?"

Suddenly Jackie's face went dark. McKinley swiveled around to see what it was she was glowering at.

"Hi, Jackie!" came a familiar voice. "Hi, Mickey! I didn't know you guys would be here!"

It was Ron, hurrying their way with a huge smile on his face. The hood of his windbreaker was pulled up to block the rain, which was really starting to pick up now.

"Hey," McKinley greeted him. "How's it go—?"

"What're you doing here?" Jackie snarled.

As usual, Ron didn't seem to notice how peeved he made Jackie, just by existing. Or maybe he took pleasure in it. It was hard to tell.

"I'm seeing *Mario*, same as you," he replied, taking his spot behind them in line. He shook out his arms, spritzing them both with rainwater. Jackie shrieked, but Ron only leaned closer, like he was about to tell them a secret. "This is my third time seeing it."

McKinley glanced at the poster again. "So it's . . . good, then?"

"Oh, no, it's terrible," Ron said. But he was smiling. *"Amazingly* terrible."

"Ugh, Ronny, you are such a"—Jackie stuck out her pointer finger and thumb like an L, then plastered it on her forehead. *"Anyway,"* she said, rolling her eyes. "Mickey and I are having an *A-B* conversation. So can you just *C* your way out, please?"

Ron held up both hands like he understood completely. "No prob," he told them. And he took the tiniest of steps backward. It was as far as he could go without leaving the awning. Jackie huffed and turned back to her book.

McKinley bit the insides of her cheeks. She hated how mean Jackie was being—but she couldn't risk saying something that might make Jackie want to marry him even less.

"As I was *saying* . . ." Jackie began, her head bent over the book. She glanced at Ron, who waved cheerfully. Jackie huffed again and thrust the book at McKinley. "I guess you'll have to read it by yourself." She pointed to the spot.

McKinley read.

> *The first film Rosas chose to screen at the newly reopened Cineplex was* Shoo, Fly! *Released in 1951, the schlocky horror film about alien arthropods who wreak havoc on an Amish community was filmed partially in Gap Bend, with several townspeople playing minor roles. In fact, many have suggested that Rosas himself must be related to the uncredited teen actor who plays "Mervin." "He does look a lot like me," Rosas admits of the actor, whose only line ("Hide the dung!")*

is perhaps the film's most infamous. "Just one of those funny Gap Bend coincidences, I guess."

"So you think," McKinley said when she finished reading, "that, um . . ." And then she trailed off. Ron was way too close for her to talk about time travel. Her eye caught on the poster beside her. "You think, um . . . *Mario* . . . traveled to, um . . ." Everything McKinley knew about *Super Mario Bros.* came from playing *Mario Kart* with Meg's younger cousins. "Rainbow Road, and ended up being in a movie, and that's what made him want to save, um, Bowser's Castle?"

Ron leaned in to tap McKinley's shoulder.

"That's not what happens in the movie, just so you know," he said. "Not to give anything away, but Mario and Luigi actually travel to Dinohattan, and Bowser is *president*, not king, so—"

Jackie cut him off with a killer glare, then turned back to McKinley. "That is what I think," she said. "And I also think there are even more, um, Marios than we know about."

Ron puffed out his cheeks. "There's only one Mario, you guys," he told them. "Are you thinking of Wario, maybe? He's sort of like Mario's evil twin, only I don't think they're actually related . . ."

Ron kept going, but McKinley wasn't listening. She knew what Jackie had been trying to say. And maybe she was right. Maybe Gap Bend was full of time travelers, just like her and Mr. Jones. McKinley glanced around, wondering how many of them might be hiding in plain sight.

20

No Rain

After Jackie paid for their tickets (and McKinley waved at Miguel, which turned out to be awkward, seeing as he had no idea who she was yet), they stepped inside the theater. Jackie didn't return to their conversation until they were at the butter station with their giant tub of popcorn.

"I think what's important," Jackie said, her voice low, "about all those people we were talking about"—*glug, glug* went the fake butter on top of the popcorn—"is that when they went back in time, they didn't hide in dumpsters like scaredy-cat Mr. Jones. They saved the town. Won contests. Got cast in movies. They *changed* stuff. Made the town better. Maybe the world, too, who knows?"

Suddenly McKinley was reminded of Aunt Connie and her C.R.A.B.S. *Better your world.* That was the fourth and—according to Aunt Connie—most important step of changing yourself. Maybe Jackie was onto something after all.

Still . . .

"I don't know," McKinley said, watching the ribbon of butter stream down. "I just wish we could know for sure who was right. That seems like enough butter."

Jackie nodded, but McKinley wasn't sure at which part.

"Hand me the salt," she instructed, and McKinley reached for the mug-size shaker.

"I don't think you can ever really know if what you're doing is the right thing or not," Jackie said, shaking out a mountain's worth of salt. McKinley was beginning to wonder if no one knew about nutrition in the '90s or if it was just Jackie who ate like this. (Neither would explain the time McKinley had witnessed grown-up Jackie eating a hot dog with Sour Patch Kids on top.) "I mean, that's true for everyone," Jackie said, "not just time travelers. So what you gotta do now is ask yourself if you're more afraid of doing something wrong—or of *not* doing something right."

McKinley found herself nodding at that. Jackie had a point—even if you *weren't* a time traveler, anything you did in life was going to lead to some kind of change. And really, there was no way for you to know what that change would be before it happened. You just had to do what you thought was right and hope for the best.

Having gotten out all her deepest thoughts, Jackie moved on to more important things. "Is this the bomb or what?" she asked, holding up the tub of popcorn. It was a greasy, salty thing of triumph.

McKinley grabbed a thick wad of napkins. "A bomb is good?" she asked.

"*The* bomb." They headed toward the door with SUPER MARIO BROS. lit up above it. "This popcorn is *the* bomb." She tossed a kernel into her mouth. "And yes."

No sooner had McKinley and Jackie stepped through the

theater door than they spotted Ron. Again. He popped out of nowhere, blocking the aisle in front of them.

"Hey, Jackie," he said, grinning. "I have something for you."

Jackie looked like she wanted to parkour off the wall to avoid talking to him, but McKinley squeezed her arm. "It won't kill you to be nice," she whispered.

And to McKinley's surprise, Jackie actually relaxed her shoulders and said, semipleasantly, "What is it?"

Ron held up a package of Tropical Skittles. "I remember once you said the mangoes were your favorite, and I think they taste like feet. So I thought maybe you'd like 'em."

For a long moment, Jackie only blinked at him. McKinley held her breath, waiting.

"Wow," Jackie said at last. "That's actually really nice, Ronny." She seemed almost pained to say the words, but still. She said them. "Thanks."

"No problem," Ron replied. A genuine smile spread across his face.

And McKinley's heart swelled up, like one of those foam crocodile toys you get as a birthday favor, the kind that grows to eight times its original size in water. Was this it? Was she witnessing the very moment when Jackie began to fall for her one true lo—

No.

No, it was not.

As it turned out, *this* was the moment when Ron put one finger to his nostril, hollered *"Special delivery!"* and, with a tremendous huff, shot a mango-flavored Skittle at his future wife . . . *straight out of his nose.*

It landed on top of Jackie's tub of popcorn, smeared in a thick coating of boogers.

"*Aaaaaaaaahhhhh!*" Jackie shrieked. Her popcorn went flying. An older lady nearby (who, McKinley would reason later, probably wouldn't have enjoyed the *Mario* movie much even without a bunch of buttery, boogery popcorn on her head) began screaming at them. And by the time the lady went to get the manager, Jackie seemed to have given up on the movie altogether.

"Come on," she said, dragging McKinley out to the lobby. Ron had ducked down into a new seat, giggling hysterically.

"But we already bought our tickets!" McKinley argued as Jackie rushed through the lobby and back into the pouring rain. In an instant, the cropped mock-neck tee McKinley had borrowed was soaked through.

"I only ever come for the popcorn anyway," Jackie replied. McKinley had to hustle to keep up with her. "And now, thanks to that turd"—Jackie jerked her head back toward the theater—"I might never eat popcorn again."

That's when McKinley knew they were in real trouble.

"Do you see what I've been telling you all this time?" Jackie went on. She plowed straight through a puddle in her pink plastic jelly sandals. "Ronny's even grosser now that I know there's a version of history where I could've ended up with him."

It was hard to argue with Jackie's reasoning. If someone popped in from the future and told McKinley *she'd* end up with Vincent Katz, the kid who put a live toad in her backpack during preschool, well . . . McKinley would want to run away from that future, too.

But McKinley knew that Ron wouldn't always be an annoying Skittle-shooting booger cannon. People changed. People—

McKinley stopped walking.

"You know," she said slowly, "I think you might be right, Jackie."

Jackie turned around. "I am?" She looked surprised.

"Yeah." McKinley nodded, making her mind up for good. "I *should* be changing things. As long as I'm here, why not make sure everything ends up a little bit better?"

And as soon as she said the words, the rain stopped. Just like that.

McKinley took it as a sign.

Jackie's face brightened, too, same as the sky. "I knew you'd come around!" she said, linking her arm through McKinley's.

But McKinley couldn't help thinking, as they made their way back to Papa Fritz's, that Jackie wouldn't be nearly so cheerful if she knew *what* McKinley planned on changing. Because like it or not, Jackie Yorks was going to end up marrying Little Ronny Rothstein.

McKinley was going to make sure of it.

21

Rock Bottom

All through school on Monday, Mr. Jones kept a creepily careful eye on McKinley, making sure she didn't do anything to upset the course of history. Every time she shifted in her seat in homeroom, he'd stop whatever he was doing to shoot eye-daggers at her. When she raised her hand in history to answer his question about the capital of Belgium, he threw up his arms and hollered, "Seriously? No one? It's *Brussels*, people!" Even in her classes with other teachers, he'd make a point to pop his head into the room and glare at her. And he wasn't exactly subtle about it. In Pre-Algebra, Miss Wormsbecker asked what she could help him with, and Mr. Jones responded, "Just checking to be sure no one is making"—he paused for a long dramatic grimace in McKinley's direction—"*history* in here."

He was giving off some serious Severus Snape vibes, McKinley thought, and not the book-seven kind.

But even a determined old crank like Mr. Jones couldn't be everywhere all the time. And so at lunch, when Ms. Friedman approached McKinley and Jackie's table to ask for extra help with the Time Hop costumes, he wasn't around to stop her.

"I know Mr. Jones said you wouldn't be joining us anymore," Ms. Friedman went on when McKinley opened her mouth to respond. "But the committee is rather desperate, and quite frankly, Mickey, you've been a godsend. I ran into Billy's mom this weekend, and she told me all about the Scarlett O'Hara dress you made from a tablecloth." She turned to Jackie, as though to emphasize her disbelief. *"A tablecloth!"* And back to McKinley: "And honestly, dear, I won't take no for an answer. So . . ." She opened up the manila folder she was holding and pulled out two crisp twenty-dollar bills. "I've decided that you and Billy may use the *very* last of the committee's funds on costumes. I thought the two of you could raid the Rock Bottom thrift shop this afternoon and see if you can find anything worth using. What do you say?"

What *could* McKinley say? If she had to choose between watching Papa Fritz read murder mysteries all afternoon or fashion hunting on the school's dime, there was really only one answer.

"I guess I wouldn't mind helping just a little bit more," McKinley told her. Jackie *ahem*-ed at her. "That is," she went on, "if you don't mind looking at the script changes Jackie and I have been working on? 'Cause some of the stuff that happened in 1939 is kinda"—how to put it delicately?—"racist and stuff? And we were thinking it'd be better to talk about it than just pretend it didn't happen."

"Mickey," Ms. Friedman replied, "if you will work your costume magic, you and Jackie can set the play in outer space."

McKinley frowned. "So that's a yes, then?" she asked.

"A big, fat yes," Ms. Friedman confirmed.

* * *

"So what'd you do to make Mr. Jones hate you so much?" Billy asked, lazily flipping through a rack of button-down shirts. He obviously hadn't been as excited about the thrift-store field trip as McKinley was.

"I didn't do anything," McKinley replied. "If you see any good floral patterns, holler, okay?"

Billy kept flipping. "It's gotta be something terrible," he said. "Because Mr. Jones hates everyone, but I've never seen him go out of his way to hate someone like *that*. In Language Arts, he told Mrs. Meucci you were 'dangerous.'"

McKinley snorted. And Mr. Jones was worried about *her* stepping on butterflies? "He thinks everyone from Colorado is dangerous," she explained. "That's where I'm from. Carbondale, Colorado." She and Jackie had decided on that location together after Jackie insisted Mickey Wells needed a backstory. They'd even looked up facts about the town in Jackie's world almanac. "It sits at the confluence of the Crystal River."

"Mmm," Billy replied. He flipped through a few more tops. "Are you gonna tell me the real reason, though? Or am I gonna have to guess?"

"No way you'd guess it," McKinley told him, grabbing for a red dress with tiny white daisies that Billy had zoomed right past. Then she noticed him smirking. "I mean . . ." She back-tracked. "Unless you guessed 'because I'm from Colorado.' Then you'd get it right away."

"Mmm," was all Billy said.

McKinley tried to ignore him. She moved past the red dress, instead tugging out a long yellow one with a thick collar. "Okay, what about this?" she asked. "It would fit Darla, and it might work for when she's supposed to be Greta Garbo." Darla Greenhalgh would turn out to be McKinley's dentist, but McKinley was trying not to get all shook about it. "Although she has to be Frida Kahlo three seconds later, so maybe that wouldn't work. Never mind."

Billy nodded for a few moments, examining the dress, before responding. "I bet you filled Mr. Jones's desk with Gak, didn't you?"

McKinley harrumphed. "I don't even know what Gak is," she told him.

"Mmm," Billy replied, his mouth an infuriating smirk.

"That's really annoying, you know," McKinley said. The dress wouldn't work. She hung it back up on the rack. "When you make that noise. It's like you're pretending to agree with me, but really you're not."

"Mmm."

"Stop it!"

"Mmm."

McKinley grabbed a pink scarf from a nearby shelf and threw it at his head. When Billy peeled it off his face, he said, "Huh." And he unfurled the scarf, examining it carefully.

"What?" McKinley asked, then immediately regretted it. He was only setting her up to say something snotty again, and she'd walked right into it.

But he didn't say anything snotty at all.

"What if Darla put this over her shoulders?" he said, turning the scarf around so McKinley could see the large colorful flowers printed on it. "It'd be like, *Wham!* Instant Frida Kahlo, right? It looks just like the sketch you drew." Then he seemed to realize he'd accidentally been helpful and scrunched the scarf into a ball.

"Wait, no!" McKinley grabbed the scarf out of his hands. "That was a really good idea." If he'd dyed his hair blue and told her he wanted to form a K-pop band, McKinley would not have been more surprised. Billy still looked annoyed at himself, though, so McKinley tried making a joke. "I mean, technically, *I'm* the one who threw it at you, so I think I should get the credit, but . . ."

Billy snorted. But all he said was, "Mmm."

Back to his normal, infuriating self.

But there was potential there. For the first time since she'd time traveled, McKinley had caught a glimpse of the awesome person Billy could be. With just a little more help.

McKinley cleared her throat. "Hey, so, I was thinking . . ."
Right your wrongs. That was step two of Connie's C.R.A.B.S.

"Did it hurt?" Billy asked her.

"Did what hurt?"

Billy smirked at her again. "When you were thinking."

In that moment, McKinley had an urge to go all *Incredibles 2* "Jack-Jack versus the raccoon" on her dad. But that wasn't going to turn *anyone* into a better person. "I was *thinking*," she said, "that when we're at your house tomorrow working on costumes you could help me bake Jackie some cookies. Butterscotch chip are her favorite."

"Why would I want to do that?"

"Because you stole her science project." McKinley picked up a pair of platform Mary Janes, more out of curiosity than anything else. Man, she had so many outfits in 2018 that these would've gone *perfectly* with. "And baking cookies seems like a nice thing to do to make up for it."

But when McKinley looked up, Billy was frowning at her like he had no idea what she was talking about.

"The *rocket ship*?" she reminded him. "You and Ron stole it before she could turn it in, and then she had to spend like the whole weekend making a new one." (In fact, it had only taken Jackie about an hour, but McKinley decided it was okay to fib for the greater good of humanity.)

"Oh, *that* science project." Billy set a fuzzy blue bucket hat on his head and struck a pose. "What do you think? Is it 'me'?"

The Jack-Jack option was getting more and more tempting. "So?" she said, trying to nudge him back to the subject at hand. "Baking cookies? You'll help me, right?"

Billy returned the hat to the shelf, between two knockoff Prada backpacks.

"Mmm," he told her.

McKinley couldn't take it anymore. "Can't you say anything?"

"Fine." Billy turned to face her, a little too close. "How about 'Right before I stole that rocket, Jackie wrote an F at the top of my homework, then told me Mr. Simonsen would thank her for saving him the trouble'? That work better for you?"

McKinley blinked. "Jackie didn't do that," she said slowly.

"Why don't you ask her?" Billy replied.

He didn't sound like he was joking.

"Okay, well . . ." McKinley let out a long, slow puff of air. "Even if Jackie did do that—"

"She did," Billy clarified. "She's had it in for me since we were in kindergarten and my mom used to babysit her. She practically ripped the skin off my arm one time." He tugged up his sleeve. "You can still see the teeth marks."

McKinley frowned. Jackie could be rude, sure, but she wasn't an arm-biting bully.

"Even if she *did* do those things," McKinley went on, "that doesn't mean you should've done something awful to her. You're in charge of what *you* do, and stealing her science project was wrong. So you ought to make up for it."

Billy picked up another hat. "So you never do anything mean when someone makes you mad?" he asked. He set the hat back down without even looking at it.

"I . . ." McKinley thought of Meg in the gym. The way her eyes had looked so wet and hurt. When McKinley got back, she'd bake Meg an entire olive loaf if it would make things right again.

(Although first she had to make sure Meg was there to apologize *to*. McKinley had been working on a plan—she just needed a little more time to pull it off.)

"Yeah," she said at last. "You're right, I do. I totally mess up and do mean things. Lots. But when I do, I try to make up for it."

Billy snorted. "Whatever, Mother Teresa," he told her. "Count me out."

"But—"

"That's a no," Billy said, "on the cookies." Then he spied something that caught his eye. "Ooh, what about this for when Ronny's being Lou Gehrig?" He pulled out a white button-down with vertical black stripes. "If we cut off the collar and add a Yankees logo?"

Suddenly McKinley felt irrationally furious about Billy's new-found passion for costuming. It was just like her dad to finally care about her interests at exactly the moment she wanted to focus on something else.

"Can you just agree that you'll *try* to be nicer to Jackie?" she growled at him. "No more stealing her stuff?"

Billy thought about it. "As long as she's not a jerk to me first," he replied with a shrug, "and it'll make you shut up."

McKinley figured that was the best she was going to get. No wrongs had actually been righted, but at least this was something she could build upon later.

. . . Or maybe there wouldn't be a later.

Because just as McKinley was telling Billy that his Lou Gehrig idea was perfect, thank you, the door to the Rock Bottom thrift store was whipped open, its bell smashing against the glass with a tremendous *CLANG!*

"*There you are!*" bellowed a voice. And every last person in the shop turned to see who had bellowed it. (One lady even peeked her head out from underneath the dressing room curtain, then quickly poked it back inside like a terrified turtle.) But once they saw him, only McKinley knew what he must be bellowing about.

"Dude," Billy whispered as they watched Mr. Jones storm closer. McKinley could feel her cheeks burning, anticipating the shouty lecture she was going to get about how dangerous it was for time travelers to shop in thrift stores. "That guy must *really* hate Colorado."

22

Revolution 1993

O nly four hours into McKinley's first day of "house arrest"
and she was already desperate to be back in school, just to
cut through the boredom. In normal times, she would've been
thrilled to skip school for four straight days. But *these* days,
McKinley didn't have her sewing machine or her phone or You-
Tube or Instagram or any of it. There was a boxy gray "Macin-
tosh Classic" computer set up in the corner of Jackie's living
room, but it wasn't connected to the internet. What was the
point of having a computer without the internet?

Worse than the boredom, though, was Mr. Jones, who had
vowed to lock McKinley in a closet until Saturday if she so much
as *thought* about leaving Jackie's house. Every thirty minutes or
so, he would call Jackie's home phone to check that McKinley
was still there. One time, McKinley had been in the bathroom when the phone rang, so he'd actually left the school to
storm over, leaning on Jackie's doorbell like a madman until she
answered.

"This isn't a joke," he'd told her, very seriously. "I need to
make sure you're not interacting with *anyone*. Do you know how
much damage you might have already caused at that thrift store
yesterday? The fate of the world is at stake."

McKinley huffed the hair out of her face. "I get that," she told her teacher. She was still wearing Jackie's Snoopy pajamas and probably starting to smell again. "But sometimes a girl's gotta pee."

So McKinley found ways to amuse herself. She raided the bookshelves and read Jackie's copy of *The True Confessions of Charlotte Doyle*. She tossed a Koosh ball up in the air to see how many times she could catch it without goofing up. (Forty-seven.) She counted how many packages of Fruit by the Foot she could find stashed inside Jackie's closet. (Nineteen.) And when she finally figured out how to use the VCR, she watched all of Jackie's taped-from-TV episodes of *Saved by the Bell*. But the whole time, McKinley was racking her brain for a way to trick Jackie into falling in love with Ron.

What McKinley needed was the perfect setup. Like when Jessie and Slater get locked in the boiler room during prom, and after a few ridiculous scenes of breaking the boiler, getting dangerously overheated, and generally wanting to murder each other, they realize that they were the perfect prom pair all along. (*Saved by the Bell* was a weird show.)

The problem was, McKinley didn't know where to find a boiler room.

And also, that sounded sort of dangerous.

It wasn't until McKinley brought her lunch—a bowl of Pizzarias Zesty Pepperoni Pizza Chips and a glass of Sunny Delight—into the living room and was booting up Jackie's Super Nintendo that she remembered what Ron had said at the Time Hop, about his and Jackie's first date.

"That's it!" she shouted excitedly, accidentally tossing the controller into the air. It landed in the bowl of chips, spraying zesty pepperoni everywhere. But McKinley didn't care. She may just have saved her best friend from nonexistence.

Jackie had a dentist appointment Tuesday afternoon. ("Sorry," Jackie told her, "but they don't let you cancel just because your daughter's best friend drops in from the future to stay with you.") So McKinley had to move Operation: Boiler Room Romance to Wednesday.

Only, when McKinley called Ron's house later—because people just put their phone numbers in giant yellow phone books, along with their *home addresses*—his older sister said Ron had kung fu on Wednesday afternoons. ("Who is this again?" Ron's sister asked. And McKinley hung up the phone in panic.)

So, Thursday it was.

"This is a great idea," Jackie said on Thursday after school. She was rewinding the tape inside her family's answering machine. "How'd you think of it?"

McKinley shrugged a shoulder. "If Kelly can leave a message on her machine telling Zack she's on her honeymoon, I figured, why can't we use yours to tell a little fib, too?"

That made Jackie laugh. "Exactly how much *Saved by the Bell* have you watched?" she asked McKinley.

"Um . . . all of it?" McKinley admitted. "By the way, someone should've really talked to the people who wrote that show about microaggressions."

"That's that thing where you say a tiny, awful thing to someone, right?" Jackie said. The tape was still whirring backward. "Like being racist or sexist or whatever without even realizing it?"

McKinley beamed at her. "Basically, yeah," she said. "See? You're getting it." McKinley had been helping Jackie all week with the script for the Time Hop play, and they had just barely finished in time for the assembly tomorrow. It wasn't that the script had been *bad*, exactly—the parts Jackie had written were especially clever and fun. It was just that everyone in the '90s apparently had a lot to learn about everything. Like, originally Jackie had cast Ron to play Mahatma Gandhi even though Ron wasn't Indian and Gandhi obviously was. And while Jackie had included tons of goofy 1939 anecdotes about Girl Scout cookies and *Superman* and Little League and the king and queen of Britain coming to the US and eating hot dogs for the first time, there was only one sentence about Adolf Hitler and the beginning of World War II. One sentence! ("But all that stuff is such a bummer," Jackie had argued. "No one wants to come to the Time Hop and learn about people being murdered. The Time Hop is supposed to be fun.")

Eventually, though, McKinley was able to convince Jackie that while the Time Hop was supposed to be a celebration of the past, it was also important to tell the truth. "Not mentioning the bad stuff doesn't make it go away," McKinley had explained. "It just makes it so kids like us don't know what really happened.

And talking about the awful stuff doesn't mean you can't talk about the good stuff that happened that year, too."

The way McKinley saw it, it was kind of her duty to speak out when she saw something that should be changed. Because she was the only person alive right now who knew how things *would* be and *could* be—and how they definitely *shouldn't* be. Mr. Jones couldn't've been more wrong about avoiding butterflies. Because if McKinley just went ahead and hid in a dumpster right now, like he thought she should, then there would never be any Meg. And if Mr. Jones was wrong about stepping on *that* butterfly, then he was wrong about all of it.

So. McKinley stepped. Everywhere she saw something awful—or even just the tiniest bit out of place—she made sure to go ahead and smush it. And as it turned out, even cooped up in your best friend's mom's childhood house for three straight days, you could make a great deal of change if you put your mind to it.

When Jackie finally had the answering machine all set up, she pressed record. "*Hello?*" she said. And she paused, waiting the length of time it would likely take Mr. Jones to growl something about McKinley. Then: "*She's still here. Now stop calling, will you?*"

She pressed save.

"How much time you think that will buy us before he figures out he's not actually talking to a person?" Jackie asked when she was done.

"Hopefully a few hours at least," McKinley said.

Hopefully, a few hours would be all she'd need. McKinley had done a good job with the Time Hop play, but there was still a lot of smushing to do.

23

Mending Fences

McKinley was thrilled when she spotted Ron and Billy inside the Galaxy Arcade.

Jackie—not so much.

"Oh, great," Jackie groaned. "Dork Brain and his idiot brother are here."

It wasn't clear to McKinley who was supposed to be Dork Brain and who was the brother, but she decided not to ask for clarification. "I thought you said Billy has been better this week," she said to Jackie. "You said all my crabbifying was working."

"I said I thought *maybe* it was working," Jackie muttered.

McKinley had moved on to checking out the arcade. "This place is awesome," she breathed. Neon stars glowed from the dark walls and ceiling. There was pinball, Skee-Ball, racing games, a prize station, and arcade games galore. It was noisy and chaotic and marvelous. "In my time, this is a furniture store." Jackie shook her head at that, like she couldn't believe what the world was going to come to. "Show me how to get quarters?"

On their way to the change machine, Ron offered them both a friendly wave, and McKinley was already patting herself on the back for getting the romance train moving.

And then Billy butted in with a blockade.

"The manager says this flyer is totally bogus," he told them, reaching Ron at the change machine just as the girls did. He was scowling at the flyer in his hand. "He said there isn't any *Street Fighter II* competition today. He said they've *never* had one."

Jackie frowned. "We got this same thing," she said, snatching the flyer. "That's why we came." She brought it closer to her nose. "You think it's fake?"

"Who would make a fake flyer?" Ron wondered.

"*Sooooo* weird," McKinley agreed—even though she knew exactly who would make a fake flyer about a fake *Street Fighter II* competition.

It turned out, annoyingly, that you couldn't just google "how to use this worthless old computer that's not hooked up to the internet," so it had taken McKinley nearly an hour to create a single shoddy-looking flyer. Then she'd had to figure out how to print two copies on Jackie's painfully slow, surprisingly loud printer and peel off the weird holey tab things stuck to the sides of each paper. She'd only barely had enough time to duck out of the house between check-ins from Mr. Jones to slip one under Ron's front door and another in Jackie's mailbox.

Jackie was already turning to leave. "If there's no prize money," she told McKinley, "then I'm outtie."

McKinley opened her mouth to give Jackie the whole speech she'd rehearsed about "Oh, please can't we stay?" and how "I've been stuck in the house for days!" and "I've never even played *Street Fighter*." But Ron beat her to the punch.

"Too afraid I'd kick your butt, huh?" he said to Jackie.

And as it turned out, that was all Jackie needed to hear.

"Oh, it is *on*," she replied, making a beeline for the *Street Fighter II* machine. Ron was right at her heels.

McKinley couldn't help but grin. Jackie and Ron had stepped straight into the boiler room without any clue about who'd sent them there.

"Shouldn't you be at home?" Billy asked McKinley. Apparently the Galaxy Arcade didn't get too crowded at 4:30 on a Thursday, so they'd managed to snag the two machines right next to *Street Fighter*. McKinley was fumbling her way through *Teenage Mutant Ninja Turtles: Turtles in Time*. Meanwhile, Billy seemed surprisingly great at *Donkey Kong*. "I mean, *I* don't want to catch your cooties."

"Uh"—McKinley glanced over at him just as he skillfully hopped over one barrel, then another—"what are you talking about?"

"Mr. Jones told us all about your head lice," Billy explained. He smashed some barrels with a hammer. "That's why you haven't been at school, right?"

McKinley pounded two buttons at once. "He's telling people I have *head lice*?" she shouted. She had no idea what the buttons did. "What the *heck*?"

Billy laughed. "I knew he was lying!" he cried. "Man, that guy hates you. What'd you do, murder his dog?"

McKinley huffed. Clearly Billy was not going to let this one go. "You really want to know why Mr. Jones doesn't like me?" she asked him.

"Yeah. And if it's something I can do, too, even better."

McKinley let go of the joystick and turned to face Billy straight on. "The reason Mr. Jones hates me," she told him slowly. Seriously. "Is because I time traveled from the future, and he's worried I'm going to upend history as we know it."

For the first time, Billy looked away from his game. "Fine," he told her. "*Don't* tell me." And then he was right back to *Donkey Kong*.

While Billy focused on climbing ladders and hopping barrels, McKinley stole glances at Jackie and Ron. She couldn't understand what anyone enjoyed about *Street Fighter*. As far as she could tell, it was just a bunch of kicking and punching. Jackie was playing as a Chinese girl with the sort of barely-there outfit that seemed much more popular in video games than in real life, and two white bun things in her hair that McKinley had never seen any Asian person wear ever. Meanwhile, Ron's character was a sumo wrestler whose arm occasionally stretched out to bizarre lengths. Jackie and Ron's smack talk was ridiculous, too. ("You're about to get hundred-hand slapped!" Ron shouted. To which Jackie replied, "Eat dirt, sumo chump!") But as soon as one game ended, Jackie slid in another quarter, and Ron didn't seem to want to stop either. So McKinley turned her attention to her other project.

"Uh, so, how's everything going with the costumes?" she asked Billy. "You ready for the assembly tomorrow?"

"I guess," he replied. *Jump-jump-climb-jump-jump.* "I got all the stuff we found at the thrift store, and my mom helped me with hems and stuff since you went and caught pretend head lice."

"I'm sorry I couldn't help more," McKinley said. "It was cool of your mom to take over. I'm sure she's really busy, with her classes and everything."

Billy shrugged, his eyes focused on the console. "It's not like it's a big deal. She loves sewing."

"Still," McKinley said. "It was a nice thing to do. And maybe you could, like, return the favor. Do you ever think about what *she* might need help with?"

"Oh, great, here comes Mother Teresa again," Billy said, rolling his eyes.

McKinley wanted to roll her eyes right back, but if she stopped paying attention to her game for one second, Leonardo would get totally pummeled by the red-headed flying bug thing, and she didn't want to run out of quarters. "No, really," she insisted. "It's important to *assess your neighbors* every once in a while." That was the *A* in Connie's C.R.A.B.S.

"What the heck does that mean?" Billy asked.

"It means . . ." McKinley tried to figure out the simplest way to explain it. "Like, take your eyes off yourself and your own problems, and see if there's anyone else in your life who could use some help."

"*You* could use some help," Billy replied.

"You know what I mean. Maybe you could"—McKinley

thought on it—"start a load of laundry for your mom sometimes. Nothing major, just a small thing to help out."

Billy rolled his eyes so hard McKinley was surprised he didn't topple over backward. "So if *you're* so helpful with all *your* laundry, then how come your parents shipped you here?"

"They didn't *ship* me here," McKinley argued. And she was about to tell Billy that she couldn't help her dad with laundry because that would disrupt his laundry schedule. (He had color-coded hampers and everything.) But their conversation was interrupted.

"Did you *see* that?" Jackie shouted, pumping one fist in the air. "Seriously, that was amazing, right? I *destroyed* you! *JACK-ee! JACK-ee! JACK-ee!*" She cupped her hands around her mouth as she chanted. "Remember that name, you guys, 'cause I'm gonna be famous for my killer moves soon. *Jackie Yorks.*" She smirked at Billy. "Want me to spell it for you? I know you have trouble sounding stuff out."

"Jackie," McKinley hissed at her. (Leonardo could fend for himself.) "Come on."

But Billy just smirked right back. "Oh, yes, please," he told Jackie. "I would *love* for you to spell it. I want to make sure I get it *just right.*"

"It's *J-A-C-K-I-E.* Ruler of All."

McKinley sighed. Who knew competition would bring out such an unpleasant side of Jackie? "Let's just go," she groaned. Now McKinley would have to come up with yet another plan to save Meg's existence—and she'd only have one day to pull it off.

But to McKinley's surprise, not everyone was ready for Jackie to leave.

"You *have* to show me how you did that," Ron said. His voice was thick with awe.

Even Jackie seemed shocked by his reaction. "Really?" she said.

"Um, of *course*," Ron replied.

And just like that, the two of them were huddled over the controls again.

"Huh," McKinley said, watching them.

"What?" Billy asked. He was back to playing *Donkey Kong*. And doing a pretty decent job, as far as McKinley could tell. It seemed like he'd gotten the high score at least a couple of times.

She blinked, not sure what to tell him. "I just . . ." Maybe love didn't always look one way or another, that's what she was thinking. Maybe there was still hope for Jackie and Ron after all. Maybe there was still hope for Meg. "I think things might actually turn out okay," she said at last.

And for the next hour or so, it seemed like they might. Until . . .

"Hey, Jackie!" It was Billy who shouted it. McKinley hadn't been paying him much attention. She was actually starting to get the hang of *Turtles in Time*. "Check this out!" Billy was practically bursting with glee. "I wanna make sure I spelled your name right."

"What are you . . . ?" Jackie destroyed Ron's character one more time, then came over to look at Billy's screen. McKinley and Ron looked, too.

Billy had been doing well in *Donkey Kong*, all right. In fact, he'd somehow earned the top five scores. But on the HIGH SCORE screen, instead of typing his initials like he was supposed to, he'd left a little message—three letters at a time, stacked down the screen. A tall, skinny insult.

```
J A C
K I E
S A H
A R Y
M A N
```

"What's a 'saharyman'?" McKinley asked, squinting at the screen. Jackie's face was flushed with anger, but McKinley wasn't sure she entirely understood why.

Ron was squinting at it, too. "*Ohhhhh*," he said, finally realizing. "'A hairy man.'"

Jackie went from red to purple.

Ron slapped Billy on the back. "I can't believe you high-scored that many times, homeslice," he said. "Only . . ." He coughed a little. "Don't you think that's sort of mean? Jackie's not even really that hairy."

"Shut up," Jackie growled.

"Yeah, we should definitely go," McKinley said. She'd never seen Jackie at a loss for words before. It was unsettling.

"No," Ron told Jackie, "I meant you have a *good* amount of hair. I like your hair."

"Stop looking at my hair!" Jackie screeched. And she folded her arms, trying to hide them between her hands and her T-shirt.

"But it's good hair," Ron argued. "It reminds me of Nitro, my aunt's dog."

And that was when Jackie slugged him. Right in the stomach.

"We're leaving now!" McKinley declared quickly, tugging Jackie by the arm. This was getting bad fast. People were beginning to stare. "Billy, you have to take that down. It's really mean."

Billy only snorted. "I couldn't even if I wanted to," he said. Ron was bent over, hands on his injured stomach. "No way I could beat all those scores. It'll probably stay like that for years."

Jackie allowed McKinley to drag her out of the arcade, but she didn't take her eyes off Billy and Ron as they went. "I hate you both!" she shouted.

"Hate you, too!" Billy called back with a jolly wave.

Ron said nothing. But McKinley caught sight of his face, and it was definitely not the face of a boy who'd just fallen in love in a boiler room. More like a boy who'd just been pushed into a boiler.

24

Burning Bridges

Why would you punch Ron?" McKinley shouted once she and Jackie were outside in the cool evening air. How on earth was she supposed to fix things now? "I can't believe you did that! You know that's your *husband*, right?"

Jackie's face had still not returned to normal. "Did you see that Billy spelled 'hairy' wrong?" she muttered. She was speed-stomping again, but McKinley was furious enough this time that she had no trouble keeping up. "I mean, of course he did. He can't even insult someone without messing up."

"Jackie, seriously. You can't just punch people."

"Oh, I barely even touched him," Jackie said, waving off McKinley's concern. "What I should've done is punched Billy, too."

McKinley could feel her own face going purple. "I get that you're mad," she said. "But that's not the way to—"

"No." Jackie stopped. Spun around on her heel. "You *don't* get it, McKinley. Because you just got here. So you didn't see all the years that your *stupid dad*"—McKinley twinged—"harassed me for wearing boy clothes or for not shaving my legs in fourth grade when all the other girls started. Like it's my fault my dad just picked out whatever he could find in the department store or that I didn't exactly feel like asking my *brand-new stepmom* how to use a razor."

McKinley frowned. "I'm really sorry, Jackie. That's awful. But I still don't think—"

"He doesn't even get how lucky he is to have a mom," Jackie went on. There were tears forming in the corners of her eyes, but McKinley was certain Jackie was too angry to let them fall. "Or how lucky he is not to remember his dad at all. I was *five* when my mom died, and I remember her, and she was *amazing*."

"Jackie." McKinley put a hand on Jackie's shoulder.

But Jackie shrugged it off. She wasn't done being angry. "And Ron just goes along with everything Billy does. He always has."

"He's going to change, though," McKinley said softly. "And you'll learn to love him, I swear."

"You don't know everything," Jackie argued.

"Um, except I actually do," McKinley snapped back. "And you keep saying that Billy's a jerk, but the biggest jerk I saw back there was you."

Jackie wiped at the corners of her eyes. Sniffled up all her tears. And when she blinked at McKinley, there was not a trace of Sad Jackie left. Only Angry Jackie remained.

Determined Jackie.

"Just because you think something," Jackie said slowly, "doesn't mean it's true." And McKinley could tell that she meant what she said—100 percent. "So you need to listen to me and actually hear me this time. I will *never* marry Ronny Rothstein. Do you understand me? Not. Ever."

And as much as McKinley wished she didn't, she believed her.

But that didn't stop McKinley, the whole walk home in silence, from planning new ways to change her mind.

25

Everybody Hurts

McKinley never imagined she'd be sneaking *into* school one day—but then again, nothing about this weird week had been close to anything she'd ever imagined before.

So there she was, Friday after lunch, slinking her way through the halls of Gap Bend Public School, doing her best to blend in with the orange lockers. If she'd timed things correctly, everyone would be at the assembly right now and all she'd have to do was sneak to Mr. Jones's homeroom and slip the note she'd written into Ron's backpack. She'd studied old homework of Jackie's all morning, until she was sure she'd gotten the handwriting just right. Then she'd folded the note into a perfect heart, the way Jackie had taught her earlier that week.

I'm sorry about how I acted. I actually think you're pretty great, and I promise to do a better job of showing it.

It wasn't much, but hopefully it could start to undo some of the damage that Jackie had caused yesterday. With any luck, if Ron thought Jackie cared about him even a little, he'd stay in the picture long enough for Jackie to come around. Jackie could be stubborn—that was clear enough from the fact that she'd refused to say a single word to McKinley from the time they'd gotten home last night until the moment they'd fallen asleep. But Jackie also had a kind heart, even if she didn't always want other people to know it. That morning, as they were brushing their teeth, Jackie had suddenly turned to McKinley and shouted, "*I'mreallysorry!*" like it was a single loud word. Then she'd side tackled McKinley with a minty-fresh hug and told her, "I'm gonna be so sad when you leave tomorrow." So McKinley had hope that Jackie could also change her mind when it came to Ron.

(McKinley, of course, had apologized, too.)

When McKinley got to Mr. Jones's door, she peered through the window into the classroom. There was Ron's desk, with his backpack slid underneath. *BINGO!* She reached into the back pocket of the cutoff jean shorts she'd borrowed from Jackie (along with a pair of ribbed black tights, a white baby doll tee, and a red plaid flannel shirt from Jackie's dad) and pulled out the note. But just as she stretched out her arm for the doorknob, she heard a voice from down the hall.

"Mickey?" McKinley turned. It was Miss Cho, the gym teacher, hustling McKinley's way. "Why aren't you at the assembly with everyone else?"

"I . . ." McKinley glanced back through the window to Ron's backpack. *So close.*

"Come on, Mickey, let's go."

McKinley sighed and slipped the note back in her shorts pocket. Once again, she was going to need to revise her plan.

* * *

"I see my class," McKinley told Miss Cho as they stepped through the gym doors. Miss Cho nodded and headed off to wherever it was she needed to be. But when McKinley tried to head back into the hall, she was stopped by another teacher, who had a pointy nose and pointier glasses.

"No one leaves till it's over," the teacher told her.

McKinley let out a quiet growl. But she made her way to a group of second graders sitting crisscross applesauce on the floor. While she moved, she kept an eye on Mr. Jones, who was way off with the rest of her class in the center bleachers. If McKinley could slip out of the gym as soon as the assembly ended, she figured she'd be able to get in and out of Mr. Jones's room without him spotting her. For now, though, there was nothing to do but sit and watch the show.

And what a show it was.

Maybe it was because of the chaos from the Sour Straw Seven's late departure from the group. Maybe it was because Jackie had rewritten the entire play from scratch—and then completely over again after getting McKinley's notes. Whatever the reason, the members of the Student Volunteer Committee looked like they'd gone on a hike in the woods without a map. Or a compass. And it was nighttime. And the woods were full of bears. And the cast members all had beef jerky in their pockets.

In other words, the play was bad.

Very, very bad.

The costumes looked great (which McKinley couldn't even really take credit for, because most of the work had been Billy's and Grandma Bev's), but the acting was stiff, and the choreography was clunky. No one knew their lines. In an attempt to solve that problem, someone had set up a projector on a wheelie cart to display the script on a white screen at the back of the gym. Every minute or so, Jackie would have to pull a sheet of transparent film off the machine and replace it with another to project the next page of lines. But that meant the entire cast kept having to twist backward, which was no one's best angle.

By the time Chanel Carlisle emerged in her checkered *Wizard of Oz* dress from the "costume corner" (which was just a rickety privacy screen from the nurse's office that the cast was attempting to change behind without knocking over), they'd completely lost the audience. The tiniest goof earned guffaws from the crowd—sometimes hoots and stomping, too. McKinley slunk down low, wishing she could melt into the floor like the Wicked Witch of the West—and take all her friends along with her.

"Why, hello, there," Chanel said, reading her lines off the projector. She was supposed to be skipping at the same time but was having trouble doing both. She skipped then spoke. Skipped then spoke. "And who might you be?"

She was speaking to Ron, who was dressed in a too-big suit with fat brass buttons. In one hand he held what appeared to be an old-fashioned radio microphone made out of a water bottle and a yardstick. In the other hand, he had an actual microphone on a cord, and he kept forgetting which one he was supposed to talk into. "Hi, Dorothy! I'm Neville Cham . . ." Ron squinted at the words on the screen. "Chamber . . ." He gave up. "The prime minister of the United Kingdom. And I'm here to declare"—just then, another kid, Reuben, leaned into Chanel's microphone to make *beep-buh-beep-beep* noises that McKinley figured were supposed to sound like something from a radio broadcast—"this country is at war with Germany!"

Chanel slapped her hands to her cheeks like that kid from the Home Alone movies. "Wow, that's big news!" she said, her words choppy as she read them off the screen. "Oh, and look! Who's this?"

There was a long pause as Jackie replaced another transparency on the projector. Then she took the microphone Reuben held out to her and said, "It's me, President Franklin—" Jackie stopped, apparently realizing that she was still dressed as Ma Joad from *The Grapes of Wrath*. She set the microphone down on top of the projector, its shadow blocking the script, and reached to the bottom of the wheelie cart to pull out a suit jacket, which she shrugged her arms into. "President Franklin D. Roosevelt!" she said at last. She clipped a tie to the front of her dress. "And guess what, everyone? I'm moving Thanksgiving! That's right, from here on out we'll all celebrate on the *fourth* Thursday of November. Isn't that a great idea?"

As Dorothy Gale and Neville Chamberlain and Franklin D. Roosevelt sat around a table to celebrate the first "Franksgiving" (along with Superman and an escapee from Alcatraz prison),

McKinley darted her eyes to the clock on the wall. When would this tragedy be over?

Around the table, the characters were discussing the trouble with the Thanksgiving story and how unfortunate it was that no people of color got to play Munchkins in *The Wizard of Oz*. Which had both been ideas McKinley suggested, but weren't working super well with the rest of the play. Jackie stood just to the side of the Franksgiving table, replacing script pages on the projector. The scene was long and boring, and the crowd was getting fidgety.

And then, suddenly, from behind the costume corner, came Billy. McKinley was surprised to see him dressed as Lou Gehrig— he probably had to switch roles last minute with Ron. He'd done a really great job on that Yankees costume, but he had a look on his face like he'd rather be diving with giant killer squid. He took the microphone from Chanel.

"Um . . ." he said, facing sideways so he could read his lines. Jackie was taking her sweet time switching the transparencies. When she finally did, the words on the page weren't typed like the other ones. They were handwritten in that pointy, up-and-down lettering McKinley had spent the whole morning studying.

I'm Lou Gehrig, the script read. *Only actually I'm Billy, and I'm so stupid I can't even read what this says.*

The audience went wild. McKinley's cheeks burned with embarrassment for her dad and her neck was twitching wildly. But Billy clearly still hadn't figured out what everyone was laughing about. He was still trying to read his lines.

"I'm Lou Gehrig," he began. He got through that part just fine, probably because he knew his character's name. Then, horribly, he leaned his face into his mic and tried to sound out the rest of the words.

"Only ah . . ." he started. "I'm ah . . ."

"Stop it!" McKinley shouted, but of course no one could hear her. All around her, kids were stomping and whooping.

"Billy," Jackie said into her own microphone. "You really can't read it, can you?" Her voice was sickly sweet. "I'll tell you what it says, then." More laughter. Even more cheering. McKinley leaped up and began to shove a path through the second graders. "It says you're stu—"

SCREECH!

That's when Ms. Friedman finally managed to yank the microphone from Jackie's hand. "That's enough out of all of you!" Ms. Friedman roared.

The room only grew louder.

As Ms. Friedman flicked off the projector, Billy stood, for one awful moment, frozen like a humiliation popsicle in the center of the gym. And then, just before McKinley could reach him, he bolted. McKinley chased after him, but she was blocked by the team of teachers trying to control the chaos. So she could only watch as he dodged through the crowd and out the gym doors.

"Hey!" There was a hand on McKinley's arm. "I can't believe you're here!" It was Jackie, and she didn't seem to care at all that she was probably going to be suspended until the invention of the iPhone. Instead, she actually looked proud of herself. "What d'you think of the changes I made to the script?"

McKinley's stomach was hotter than a bowl of overmicro-waved oatmeal. "Are you *kidding* me right now?" The principal had gotten on the mic, shouting at everyone, but it wasn't helping. "That wasn't okay!"

Jackie stuck her hands on her hips. "Sorry I didn't check with you about it first," she snapped.

"What does that mean?" McKinley asked.

"It means," Jackie told her, "that you have to be in charge of everything. You think you're smarter than everyone else and everyone should do exactly what you say."

"What?" McKinley said. "I do not!"

Jackie snorted. "Right. So it *wasn't* you who's been telling me who I should marry? Who I'm supposed to turn into? How my whole life is supposed to be?"

McKinley threw up her arms. "I'm not trying to be in charge," she argued. "I just know how things are supposed to be. I've been trying to *help* you!"

Jackie glared at McKinley. "You know who you sound like right now?"

McKinley blinked.

"Mr. Jones," Jackie told her.

"What? I'm nothing like—"

"You both think you know exactly how the world should be. And if anyone tries to do anything different, you freak out."

"Well, when you try to do things *your* way," McKinley argued, "you do stuff like *this*." She waved her arms, indicating the chaotic mess that was this assembly. Her dad's humiliation.

"You know what?" Jackie shot back. "You should just go and stay with your best friend Mr. Jones tonight." Her voice was sharp. "'Cause you're definitely not staying with me. I'll be so glad when you leave tomorrow."

McKinley felt the back of her neck go hot. "Fine," she said. "I wouldn't want to stay with you anyway. All you are is a jerk and a bad writer." Jackie's face crumpled at that. McKinley's dart had hit her hard—that was obvious. But McKinley wasn't letting her off that easy, not after what Jackie had just done. "I used to think you were so cool," she told Jackie. "Hanging out with me and Meg like you were our friend instead of a boring old mom." She spotted Mr. Jones then, making his way toward them. He had seen her, clearly, and he probably thought this whole thing was her fault. "But now I know that it's just because even when you're a grown-up, you can't find any friends of your own. No one likes you, Jackie. Not now, not ever."

And before Jackie could find any words to shout back at her, McKinley turned. And she ran.

26

Already There

At the back of the school, in the corner of the track field, was an equipment shed whose lock was nearly always undone. McKinley knew that because sometimes, when she and Meg were supposed to be running the mile, they'd sneak inside and listen to songs on Meg's phone (Meg always had the best playlists). They'd squeeze themselves against the dark wall, butts on the dusty floor, sharing a pair of earbuds for two full songs. Then, reluctantly, they'd hoist themselves up and return to the field, shrugging their shoulders at Mr. Halifax when he wondered why their times were always so slow.

That's where McKinley headed now. The shed, she discovered, wasn't locked in this millennium either. She slipped inside and closed the door almost-but-not-all-the-way shut, so a sliver of light crept across the floor. And she kept one eye on the field outside, worried and waiting.

McKinley took a deep, calming breath. *In. Out.* It smelled like rubber and dirt inside, just the same as always. *In. Out.* It was strangely comforting.

It took a few minutes, but eventually Mr. Jones did pass the shed. McKinley clenched her stomach until the teacher and his scowl were out of sight. Then, with a sigh of relief, she plopped herself down on a medicine ball in the middle of the shed.

And she began to cry.

"You okay?"

McKinley startled so badly she fell right off the ball, smacking to the ground.

"Jeez. It was just a question."

In the sliver of light, McKinley could only barely make out Billy's red-brown hair. He was standing in the long shadows of two equipment shelves. "You scared me!" she shouted, wiping all evidence of tears off her face.

Billy held up his hands like he hadn't meant to cause trouble. "Sorry," he told her. "I just heard you crying, and—"

"I wasn't crying," McKinley snapped.

"Okay," he replied. He didn't believe her.

"I didn't know you were in here," McKinley said next.

Billy shrugged his shoulders. "I didn't know where else to go," he said.

McKinley climbed back onto her medicine ball, and to her surprise, Billy pulled up a basketball next to her. But he didn't say anything. They sat in silence for a long time, rolling slightly this way and that, each of them thinking their own thoughts. McKinley picked at a loose thread on the knee of Jackie's black tights, even though she knew it would make a hole. Billy stared at a rack of lacrosse sticks.

After a while, though, McKinley couldn't take the silence anymore. *Someone* had to talk, and McKinley figured it might as well be her.

"I'm sorry that happened to you." That's what she decided to say.

Billy kept staring. Didn't even blink. "It wasn't your fault," he said.

"No," McKinley agreed. "But . . . it shouldn't've happened. That was awful."

He let out a soft grunt, like, *What are you supposed to do?*

They were silent again.

Until, suddenly, Billy sucked in his breath. "No *way!*" he cried, excited. And he jumped off his ball to examine something on one of the bottom shelves.

"What is it?" McKinley asked.

Billy didn't answer. Instead, he grabbed at a pile of what looked like tiny cough drops and chucked one at the ground. It *CRACKED!* when it hit, and there were sparks, too—a miniature explosion.

"Sweet!" Billy said. He tossed some more.

CRACK!

BANG!

POP!

"What *is* that?" McKinley was up on her feet now, flinching with every miniature blast.

"They don't have snaps where you're from?" Billy asked.

"Snaps?"

"Poppers," he told her. "Whiz-bangers. Whip'n pops."

"What are you talking about?"

Billy held them out for her to see—small twists of dirty paper. But when she came closer, he tossed the whole handful at her feet.

The crackle of tiny thunderclouds sent McKinley dancing backward. She took a moment to catch her breath while Billy doubled over in laughter. "Are you for real right now?" she screeched at him.

"You should see your face!" he cackled.

"You could've killed me."

"Oh, please," Billy scoffed. "They sell these in the toy aisle. There's barely even any gunpowder in them."

"Gunpowder?" If McKinley's father ever caught her playing with gunpowder, she'd be grounded until she forgot what the sun looked like.

Billy was busy stuffing the rest of the snaps into his pockets.

"Be careful you don't burn your butt off," McKinley advised.

Billy rolled his eyes. "Don't you have somewhere to be?"

"Not . . . really," McKinley admitted. She was probably going to have to spend the night in this shed. She definitely wasn't going back to Jackie's. McKinley squinted at Billy. "It was inexcusable," she said. It was a word her dad would've used.

"Huh?"

"What Jackie did." McKinley still couldn't wrap her head around it. "I mean, who makes fun of someone's dyslexia in front of the whole school?"

Billy was staring at her without even blinking. It was kind of creepy.

"Are you gonna throw more snaps at me?" McKinley asked him.

"I don't have dyslexia," he replied.

"You don't have to be embarrassed," McKinley told him. "A lot of people have it. My friend Meg has something sort of similar, and she figured out all these cool ways to—"

"No." Billy was firm this time. "I mean, I *really* don't have it. Who even told you that?"

"Of course you . . ." McKinley trailed off, then tilted her head to one side. "Wait a second. When do you get diagnosed?"

"Huh?"

Was it possible he didn't know yet? But how had he gotten through school this whole time?

"Okay," McKinley said. "On Monday, you gotta go to Mrs. Elkins." He kept staring. "Or, um, whoever the counselor is now. Tell them you want to get tested for dyslexia."

Billy finished stuffing his pockets. "Yeah, no thanks," he said. He crossed to the shed door, checked both ways, then slid outside.

McKinley slid out right behind him. "Seriously," she told him, "you have to get tested. It'll help a lot, I promise."

"I'm just fine without your help, weirdo." Billy was crossing the track field now, on his way to the gate at the far end.

McKinley crossed the field, too.

"You have trouble remembering the order of things, right?" she called as he raced off ahead of her. "And spelling is really hard? And sometimes you mix up your letters?"

Billy stopped. Turned around slowly.

"How do you know that?" he asked.

McKinley caught up with him. "Once they diagnose you, there's lots of stuff the teachers can do. You'll get extra time on tests, and you might be able to listen to audiobooks instead of reading. It'll make a big difference. You should really talk to the counselor."

He turned back around. "Maybe," he said.

But at least it wasn't a no.

The gate was locked, but Billy hopped over easily.

McKinley hopped over, too, not so easily.

"You can't go home, you know," McKinley said when he went to turn onto Clover Street. "It's only twelve. If your mom finds out you ditched, she'll murder you."

Billy stopped. "If you're so worried about getting in trouble," he grumbled, "why don't *you* go back to school?"

"I'm not supposed to be there anyway," McKinley replied. "Head lice and all that."

Billy's eyebrows knit themselves together. "You're weird," he told her.

"You have no idea."

And then, suddenly, McKinley had a thought.

"I know where we can go," she said. She jerked her head toward Hotch Avenue. "Come on. You'll like it."

Maybe McKinley hadn't done anything she'd planned on doing that morning. And maybe she'd even made everything worse. But that didn't mean her final few hours had to be a total bust.

27

Jurassic Park

W ell, aren't you two in luck?" Miguel said when they popped their heads above the ticket window at the theater. "First people at the first screening. You get whatever seats you want. I'm actually shocked there isn't a line around the block already. But I guess some kids are still in school."

"Um . . ." McKinley began.

But Miguel only laughed. "Don't worry," he said, handing over their tickets. "I once cut class to see *Ghostbusters*."

After they snagged the perfect seats—middle row, center— McKinley dug into the popcorn. As soon as this movie was over, she decided, she'd race over to Ron's house. She'd tell him she'd come to say goodbye, maybe, since she was heading home tomorrow—and while she was there, she'd slip in some awesome facts about Jackie, just to keep it in Ron's head that she might one day be soulmate material. (Even though McKinley wasn't exactly feeling like Jackie's biggest cheerleader at the moment, she'd dig extra deep to think of awesome things to say about her if it meant saving Meg. Meg was too incredible not to ever be born.)

She glanced at Billy chomping on handfuls of popcorn. Not even noticing the bits of kernels speckled across his shirt. When

McKinley got home tomorrow, would she even recognize her dad? Would he be a completely different, amazingly understanding and chill father? Or had she not done enough, yet, to change him?

"So, um, remember that thing that happened at the assembly?" McKinley said. "With, uh, Jackie?"

Billy kept his eyes on the ad for the Sunny Acres Retirement Center displayed on the movie screen. "Yep," he said, reaching for more popcorn. "I was there."

"Yeah, of course," McKinley replied. "I was just thinking . . . wouldn't it be great if you, like, took this awful thing that happened to you and used it to make the world a better place?" *Better your world.* That was number four on the list. "Like, you could start a program to stop bullying, or make sure kids with dyslexia can get diagnosed early. It'd be like your Batman moment."

"My what?"

"Like when Batman's parents die right in front of him, but instead of turning into some sort of supervillain because of it, he decides to do something positive for the rest of the world." Was it possible Billy didn't even know the Batman story? Hopefully today's little field trip would start him down the path of more regular movie-going. "That's why Batman starts fighting crime."

Billy crunched silently on his popcorn for so long that McKinley began to wonder if she'd been speaking out loud.

"Um, hello?" she said.

Billy took a long, loud gulp of soda, then slid it back into the cupholder between them. "Being a supervillain doesn't seem that awful," he said at last. "At least the Joker doesn't have to dress like a bat. Bats are gross."

So apparently he knew about Batman after all.

McKinley pinched the bridge of her nose the way her dad sometimes did when he was growing frustrated. "You are totally missing the—"

"I'm just saying it's too late for me," Billy told her. He was spraying bits of popcorn as he spoke, and McKinley was pretty sure it was on purpose. "Because my dad already died, remember? And it just turned me into *this*."

McKinley's cheeks went hot. Why had she decided to talk about dead parents? "Sorry," she said. "I didn't mean—"

"It's fine," Billy told McKinley. He honestly seemed more focused on devouring all their popcorn before the previews started. But then he glanced sideways at her. "Is that why *you're* here?" he asked.

"Huh?"

"Did your parents croak, too?" Billy said. "It would explain why you moved across the country all by yourself."

"My parents aren't dead," McKinley said. (Which, she realized, was a weird thing to say to your own dad.)

"Oh," Billy replied. He grabbed another handful of popcorn. "So they must hate you, then."

"What?"

"If they shipped you here."

The screen in front of them flipped to an advertisement for Larry's Music Land. "They don't hate me," McKinley said.

"Mmm," Billy replied.

"They *don't* hate me. My dad . . ." McKinley blinked. "Well, he doesn't get me. But he doesn't *hate* me."

Billy snorted.

"What?" McKinley asked.

"Maybe you're just hard to get," he said.

McKinley growled and reached for the popcorn.

Billy yanked the tub away. "What about your mom?" he asked. "Are you guys, like, best friends who paint your toenails together every night or whatever girls do?"

When McKinley managed to grab the popcorn back, she tucked the tub in the crook of her arm, where Billy couldn't reach it. "My mom is my mom," she said. There was really no other way to describe it. "She's great, I love her, but . . ."

"Yeah?"

McKinley always had trouble explaining her mom, even to people like Meg. "Okay, so my parents split up when I was two, right?" she said. Billy nodded, actually paying attention for once. "And I always just lived with my dad. Which kind of made me mad for a while, because my mom is so fun and interesting and weird. And my dad is . . ." She tried to think of the right word, and then settled on the simplest. *"Not."*

"So why don't you move in with your mom, then?"

"Parents don't let you pick that kind of stuff for yourself," McKinley replied. "They always think they know what's best for you. Anyway, I see my mom a lot, but she travels so much for work that it's usually just a couple days. Only, this one time—I was eight, I think—I finally got to spend the whole summer with her."

"And it was awful?" Billy guessed. When McKinley tilted her head at him, confused, he explained: "It just seemed like that's where your whole boring story was going."

McKinley narrowed her eyes at him while she decided whether or not she should keep going. It was hard enough to talk about this stuff to anyone, let alone to someone who was being all *Billy* about it. But in the end, she decided she might as well finish the story. She'd be leaving tomorrow, anyway.

"It was awesome, actually," she went on. "We watched tons of TV and made forts in the living room to sleep in, and we didn't follow a meal schedule or anything. Sometimes she'd take me out for Froyo at lunchtime, and then for dinner we'd just eat salami slices and pickles straight from the jar."

"What's Froyo?" Billy asked.

"Frozen yogurt."

"Oh." He nodded. "Well, that does sound pretty cool."

"I loved it," McKinley said. "And my mom loved being with me, too, I could tell. But . . ." She searched for the words. "She didn't have any spoons."

"Huh?" Billy asked.

"One day my mom decided we should make pumpkin soup, from scratch. She'd found a recipe onli—er, in a book—and she wanted to cook it. So we walked to the farmers market and got all the ingredients, and we spent *hours* making it—scooping out the pumpkin guts with our hands, slicing it up, roasting it, making this huge batch of soup. And then, when we were all done—it was like ten o'clock at night—my mom realized she didn't have any spoons to eat it with."

"How does someone not have spoons?"

"She said she must've only ever cooked food that used forks," McKinley said. "So I ate my soup with the spatula we'd used to stir the pot, and my mom kept dipping in this one chopstick. It was pretty ridiculous. Finally, when it cooled down enough, we poured the soup into mugs and drank it." McKinley took a handful of popcorn from the tub then stared at it in her hand for a moment. "That's just the kind of person my mom is, I guess."

"The kind without spoons?"

McKinley nodded.

Billy thought about that. "It doesn't seem like the worst thing," he said. "She's cool and she loves you. So what if she doesn't own spoons?"

"Yeah," McKinley agreed. "Sure. But . . ." For some reason, even though it wasn't a *bad* memory, exactly, she didn't like this next part. "Well, okay, a couple weeks after I got back to my dad's, it was her birthday, right? So I mailed my mom this big box of plastic spoons. Wrapped it in birthday paper and everything. Sort of like our inside joke, you know? Only, the next time I went to visit her, which was like four months later, she hadn't opened the box."

"She didn't unwrap your present?" Billy asked. "Rude."

"No." McKinley wasn't telling it right. "She'd unwrapped it—she just hadn't taken the spoons out. I had to ask her where they were, and it took her forever to find them. She'd shoved them up in some cabinet with a dusty punch bowl. It was like she didn't even *want* to own spoons." McKinley took in a deep, calm breath. *In, out.* As hard as it was to share, it felt good getting the spoons story off her chest. She was glad she'd finally told someone. "That's when I knew I was better off living with my dad, even if he was, well, *him*."

Billy was staring at her again. She didn't like it.

"*What?*" she asked.

"You're the worst," he told her. Then he grabbed the popcorn tub from her armpit and went back to stuffing his face.

McKinley was mad now, for real. Of *course* Billy would go and be a jerk, right when she'd opened up. "I don't know why I thought you'd understand," she told him. "You never do."

"Oh, I understand fine," he said. Calm as ever. *Crunch crunch.* "You tried to change your mom, and it didn't work, and you got mad. Classic Mickey." *Crunch crunch.*

"What do you mean, 'Classic Mickey'?"

Billy shrugged. "You come to our town out of nowhere, act like you know everything about everyone, and then try to change everything to the way *you* think it should be."

"I don't—"

"Maybe some people just like using forks," he said. The lights were beginning to dim. For the first time, McKinley noticed that the theater was stuffed with people. "Ever think of that?"

McKinley huffed. "I didn't want to *change* her," she argued. "I just thought she needed spoons."

"She never needed them before," Billy pointed out.

"But *everyone* has spoons," McKinley argued. "It's weird not to have them."

"Mmm," Billy said, like she'd made his point for him.

McKinley huffed again.

"Were the spoons your Batman moment?" Billy asked. The trailers were starting, but he didn't bother to lower his voice. "Did you open up a charity for kids who don't know how to eat soup?"

McKinley's stomach felt sour. He'd gotten it all wrong—twisted up her story so she was the villain somehow. "You are a *horrible* person," she told him. She couldn't believe she'd thought for a second he'd understand anything about her.

From one row back, a man leaned forward to bark at them. "Are you kids planning on talking through the whole movie?"

Billy turned around in his seat. "Probably," he told the man. "See, I'm a horrible person, and her"—he pointed—"she's the worst."

McKinley made fists so tight her fingernails bit her skin. "Shut *up*," she told Billy.

The man behind them stood. "I'm getting the manager," he said, but the woman beside him tugged on his arm. He sat back down, but he didn't look thrilled about it.

McKinley squashed herself down in her seat, like she could squash up her feelings that way, too. "Just be quiet," she whispered to Billy. "I don't want to get kicked out."

"*Or*," Billy whispered back, bumping her shoulder, "we could give that guy a really good reason to kick us out."

McKinley wouldn't look at him. "Watch the movie, would you?"

"Mmm," he said.

McKinley ignored him all through the trailer for some movie called *Last Action Hero*. She ignored him through the next one, too, and the next one, even as he poked her with his elbow while he was digging something out of his pocket. Even as he hogged all the popcorn in the tub. Even as he slurped his soda so loudly she thought the guy behind them might die coughing.

And at last the movie began. McKinley felt her stomach settle as the menacing music started up. The raptor was clearly gonna eat one of those dudes, and she was really looking forward to it.

Billy elbowed her in the arm again.

"Stop hogging the armrest!" McKinley hissed, pushing back against him.

He elbowed harder.

"What?" McKinley snapped, finally turning to look at him.

In the eerie light from the movie screen, Billy's grin looked downright villainous. "Wanna make the guy behind us pee his pants?" he whispered. He pointed to the floor in front of them.

It was dark in the theater, and at first McKinley thought that it was only spilled popcorn, what Billy was pointing to. And then he raised his leg, hovering over the thirty or so popcorn-size balls like he was going to smash them, and her eyes went wide in horror.

They were snaps.

Poppers.

Whip'n pops.

"*Billy, no!*" McKinley hollered. She grabbed his arm, hard, to stop him from setting them all off.

"That's it!" the guy behind them huffed, already squeezing his way into the aisle.

Billy was laughing his head off. "*Psych!*" he told McKinley. "Like I'd waste any snaps on that guy."

"Just put them away," McKinley snarled. "You're ruining the movie."

"You're such a buzzkill," Billy told her. He shoved the almost empty popcorn tub into her lap and bent down to get the explosives.

Only, he must've bent a little too fast, because his face met the seat in front of him with a sharp *CRACK!* He screamed so loudly that at least three new people shushed them.

"Don't be such a baby," McKinley said. "You're totally f—"

When Billy pulled his hand away from his face, she saw the blood. Lots of blood. Like, a-T.-rex-chomped-off-your-nose amounts of blood.

"I think it's bleeding," Billy whimpered.

"Shoot." McKinley gave him all the crumpled-up napkins she had. But no sooner had he pressed them to his face then they turned a dark, soggy red. "Maybe we should leave," McKinley said. "I think your nose might be bro—"

McKinley's whole body went cold.

"Mickey?" Billy asked. She couldn't move. "Mickey? What's wrong? You're freaking me out."

On screen, the raptor was totally eating that dude. Peals of screams bellowed from the theater's speakers, and from the audience, too.

"We have to go to your house, Billy," McKinley said. *"Now."* And she didn't wait for him to argue, didn't even let him grab more napkins from the concession stand on the way out. "There isn't time," she kept saying.

Because she'd been wrong all along. It wasn't her dad she'd needed to change. Or Jackie, either.

"There isn't any time."

The one thing McKinley should've been trying to prevent—the only thing that mattered—had been right in front of Billy's not-yet-broken nose all along.

McKinley spotted the ambulance outside their house as soon as they turned the corner. There was Aunt Connie, freaking out, flustered like McKinley had never seen her, hollering at an EMT. And there—McKinley's whole heart collapsed when she saw her—was Grandma Bev, being pulled from the house on a stretcher, an oxygen mask covering her face.

"Mom?" Billy said, taking in the scene. His face was smeared with dried blood. It was all down his shirt, his arm, everywhere. "What's going on?"

They were too late. McKinley had gotten there too late. And now things were only about to get worse.

Come Undone

The hospital smelled like floor cleaner and desperation. McKinley wasn't sure how long she and Billy had been sitting in that waiting room. Nine years, it felt like. They didn't talk much, just tried different ways to scrunch themselves into the weird boxy chairs. *Who would make a chair with a padded back and wooden arms?* McKinley wondered after the sixteenth time she pinched her funny bone. Either you wanted a comfy chair, in which case you should pad all of it. Or you wanted an uncomfortable one, in which case you should pad none of it. Only padding part of a chair just seemed cruel—like you were trying to lure people into taking a nap so that as soon as they began to drift off—*WHAM!*—they'd hit their ear on a sharp corner. McKinley finally pulled over a second chair, thinking that maybe she could push two horrible chairs together to make a semihorrible chair boat. At least then she could put her feet up.

She noticed Billy watching her, and he looked so awful, with the dark circles under his eyes and the purple bruises on either side of his poor crooked nose, that McKinley got him another chair, too. He offered her a half grunt as he stuck his feet up, which McKinley took to mean *Thank you.*

Billy hadn't said much on the ambulance ride over. Aunt

Connie had been allowed to ride in the back with Grandma Bev, but the EMT made McKinley and Billy sit up front with him. The EMT tried to joke about the Phillies, but Billy was in some sort of daze and didn't even seem to hear him. Meanwhile, McKinley couldn't stop blinking. It was the only thing she could think to do that might clear away the image of Grandma Bev on that stretcher.

Her hair all out of place.

Her skin pale.

It shouldn't have been such a shock, really. Obviously McKinley had always known about Grandma Bev's stroke. But there was something very different about knowing a thing and experiencing it. Like how you know it must hurt to break your arm, but then when it happens, you realize that there aren't even words to describe how painful it can be. Now that McKinley had gotten to know the Grandma Bev who existed before, her stroke seemed like a whole different event. Like Grandma Bev hadn't just lost some words and her right hand when she got sick—she'd lost her future, too. What would've been, if not for this.

And for the first time, it occurred to McKinley that maybe her dad had lost the same thing.

McKinley curled up tight in her chair boat, trying to squeeze her guilt away. If only she hadn't been so wrapped up in the things she thought she *should* be changing, she would've known to be at the house that day. Maybe then she would've been able to change the one thing that actually mattered. She went to wipe away a tear she didn't even deserve to be crying—and accidentally smacked her wrist on the inside edge of the chair arm.

"*Frosted monkeys!*" McKinley shouted. It was something she and Meg had started saying as a joke, instead of cursing, and then somehow ended up using for real.

To McKinley's surprise, she heard a soft chuckle from the chair boat beside her. She swiveled her head to peek at Billy.

"Sorry," he said, swiping his nose with the back of his hand. "I wasn't laughing because you got hurt. It's just . . . I think these chairs were designed by the devil."

McKinley shifted herself to sitting. "Right?" she said.

"I almost gouged my eye out like four times," Billy replied. "I bet half the people getting surgery right now started out in this waiting room."

It was McKinley's turn to laugh. "Maybe that's how they make sure they have enough patients."

They were quiet again for a while after that, but it was a more comfortable quiet. They sat back in their chair boats watching an infomercial for spray-on hair on the TV above their heads.

When Billy finally did speak, his voice was soft.

"When do you think they'll let me see her?" he asked.

"I'm not sure," McKinley answered. They'd gotten updates, for a while, when Aunt Connie was still in the waiting room with them. A nice nurse had taken Billy to get his nose checked out and to change his bloodstained shirt. He'd come back not long after with an ice pack and a T-shirt the nurse found who knows where that said D.A.R.E. TO KEEP KIDS OFF DRUGS. But then Grandma Bev had been moved to a new ward, and Aunt Connie was allowed to go in and visit—and McKinley and Billy had just been left sitting there. Sometime around what felt like the turn of the last century, the waiting room had cleared out, and the ice pack had melted into a puddle pack, and McKinley and Billy hadn't seen a single other person since. McKinley wasn't sure if that was because it was the middle of the night (maybe?) or because no one really bothered to update kids. "I can go check with someone." She started to push away the foot part of her chair boat, but Billy shook his head.

"No, it's okay," he said. "I'm not even sure I want to see her." As soon as he said it, he darted his eyes toward his lap. "I didn't mean . . ."

But McKinley understood. "I'd be freaked out, too," she told him. "If it was my mom."

Billy sniffled. "Thanks," he said, his eyes back on the TV. "For staying with me while . . ." He didn't seem to want to finish the sentence.

"Of course," McKinley replied. She knew she didn't deserve to be thanked, but there was no way to explain that to Billy. Anyway, it hadn't occurred to her that she could leave. Thankfully, no one had asked her to. The nurses had assumed she was Billy's sister, and Aunt Connie had been so frantic making phone calls—to everyone from their bridge-club members to Grandma Bev's insurance—that she never looked up long enough to wonder why McKinley was there. "I'm sorry I couldn't stop it."

Billy turned to her, confused. "How could you have stopped it?" he asked.

And since she couldn't exactly tell him the truth, McKinley decided to tell him something else.

"I'm leaving tomorrow," she said. "Like, for good. I have to go home."

Billy suddenly seemed fascinated by the skin around his left thumb. He picked at it. "To your dad?" he asked.

McKinley nodded.

"That's cool, I guess," Billy replied. "I bet you're glad to get out of here."

McKinley thought about that. "Yes and no," she said. She was sick of talking about sad things. She wondered, for a moment, if she should go back to trying to crabbify Billy. But then she remembered that the next letter in Connie's C.R.A.B.S. was S, for *Shake up your routine.* And she decided that Billy's routine was about to get shaken up enough. So instead, McKinley wiggled out of her boat to grab something she'd spotted on one of the end tables across the room.

"What's that?" Billy asked as she crossed back to him.

"Deck of cards." McKinley showed him. "Someone must've left it. Wanna play Spit?"

"Uh, what?"

"The game," McKinley clarified. "Spit." Billy still seemed confused. Which confused *McKinley* because he was the one who'd taught it to her—way back when they still did things like play cards together. She dragged over an end table with a shriek that was much too loud for Whatever O'Clock in the morning. "I'll teach you."

And there was a small stretch of time while they were playing cards that they could forget why they were in that hospital.

Well, maybe not *forget*, exactly, but just stay in a state of half-knowing. Like a cicada buried deep underground in its beautiful snooze, dreaming about whatever cicadas dream about—molting, maybe—but still aware, in the back of its little buggy mind, that sooner or later it was gonna have to come bursting out of the ground in a great terrifying swarm and eat everything it sees and leave a freaky little buggy case of itself on a fence post to traumatize children everywhere. It might've seemed peaceful at the moment, but you still knew chaos was looming.

It wasn't until the infomercials shifted into early-early morning news shows that McKinley began to notice her stomach growling. She glanced at Billy, who was attempting to shuffle the deck.

"You hungry?" she asked, grabbing the cards from him. Man, he was bad at shuffling. She flipped the cards together easily. "I could check if the cafeteria's open."

He blinked, like hunger had just occurred to him. "Actually, yeah," he said. "I haven't eaten anything since that popcorn." He blinked again. "I hope whoever had to sweep up the theater didn't get *too* freaked out by those snappers."

McKinley put a hand to her mouth. "I didn't even think of that! I wonder if the guy's here right now, after his heart attack." She was laughing, but not. It wasn't funny, really—but anything was funnier than thinking about Grandma Bev in her hospital bed. (What was Grandma Bev thinking about? She must be so scared. McKinley shook the thought out of her head.)

Billy grimaced. "Maybe I should, like, send them an anonymous sorry note or something."

"Righting your wrongs," McKinley said. "Nice."

And Billy must've been feeling more like himself again, because he rolled his eyes at that.

"See if they have Frosted Flakes," he said, tossing her the "emergency cash" Aunt Connie had left them.

"Sure," McKinley told him.

Grabbing Frosted Flakes seemed like the least she could do.

29

The Key, the Secret

They didn't have Frosted Flakes, so McKinley decided to get omelets. She ordered bacon and cheese for herself and a southwest for Billy, hoping he had the same taste buds as he would when he was thirty-seven. But by the time she got back to the waiting room on the third floor, Billy wasn't there. She walked all the way back to the elevator, clutching her tray, just to make sure she'd gotten off on the right floor, then to the waiting room again. She was still standing there, staring at the empty chair boats, when a nurse walked by.

"You okay, sweetheart?" the nurse called over.

Maybe it was because she was extra tired or because it was thirteen years before she was even supposed to be born or because hospitals just made you a little loopy, but whatever it was, McKinley couldn't find the words to explain her situation. "I got omelets," she said. "But my dad . . . I mean, my brother . . ."

The nurse seemed unfazed. McKinley wondered if she saw a lot of confused kids holding breakfast trays. "Come with me," she said. "We'll figure out where your family is."

Five minutes later, the friendly nurse, Lydia, led McKinley into room 516, just a few doors down the hallway. "I found someone who belongs to you," Lydia told the room.

But McKinley couldn't move. Just stood in the doorway, holding on to her tray of omelets. There was Aunt Connie, in the chair facing the door, wide-eyed and ready for action. Billy, sitting beside her, his shoulders slumped. And Grandma Bev, lying in the hospital bed, blinking at the ceiling, hooked up to who knows what. Every other second, one of the machines let out a tiny beep, like it wanted to remind them all where they were.

Lydia took the tray from McKinley and set it on the counter beside the sink. "It always looks worse than it is," she whispered, "first time you see 'em." She put a hand on McKinley's back and nudged her toward the empty chair in the corner, the same horrible kind from the waiting room. "She's still the same lady you've always known, I promise."

McKinley plunked her butt down in the seat. She didn't look at Billy, didn't say anything. She only stared at Grandma Bev's pale face and matted, sweaty hair. Half her grandmother's face was sagging—the right side—just the way McKinley had always known it. But now it looked wrong.

At some point, Lydia must've left the room. McKinley didn't even notice. It took McKinley a long time, too, to notice that Aunt Connie was being a little too . . . Aunt Connie.

"You gotta eat," Aunt Connie was telling Grandma Bev. She was perched on the edge of her chair, holding a bowl of oatmeal, with a too-full spoon dripping back into the bowl. Aunt Connie kept trying to jab the spoon into Grandma Bev's face, and Bev kept jerking away, squinching her eyes closed. "The doctor said if you can't eat on your own, they're gonna have to put you on a feeding tube, and I *know* you don't want that. Come on, just try." And that time she crammed the spoon into Grandma Bev's mouth before Bev could dodge away. "There you go. It's good, ri—?"

Before Aunt Connie finished her sentence, Bev coughed, sputtering out all the oatmeal.

"Oh, for Pete's sake!" Aunt Connie shouted. She stood to flick oatmeal spray off her rumpled shirt.

Billy was up on his feet, too. "You're *choking* her," he cried. And he moved like he was going to pat his still-coughing mother on the back but couldn't quite shift his hand into the right spot. "We gotta get the nurse."

"She's fine," Aunt Connie snapped. "She's just being stubborn. Doesn't know perfectly good oatmeal when she tastes it." McKinley knew Aunt Connie was probably tired, too, and just as scared as any of them, but it was hard not to want to shake her right now.

McKinley glanced from Billy to Grandma Bev to Aunt Connie. One looked terrified, the other stunned, the last one ready to wrestle a wolf with her bare hands. But the one thing they all had in common, McKinley realized, was that they all seemed completely helpless. And when she realized *that*, suddenly McKinley wasn't the awkward kid with the tray of omelets anymore. For maybe the first time in this whole bizarre time-travel experience, she knew exactly what to do.

"I saw some smoothies in the cafeteria," McKinley told Aunt

Connie, jumping into action. "Maybe that would be easier for her to eat?"

Aunt Connie blinked at McKinley a few times, and McKinley held her breath, but finally she took the bait. "Would that be good, Your Highness?" Aunt Connie asked Grandma Bev. And McKinley knew if her grandmother had had the strength, she absolutely would've swatted Aunt Connie right about then. "If that doctor comes in while I'm gone, tell him to wait for me. I have about fifty questions to ask him, and he's not going to weasel away again."

As soon as Aunt Connie was out of the room, McKinley hopped up to grab some paper towels, then got to work cleaning Grandma Bev's oatmealy chin.

"You think the smoothie will work?" Billy asked. He was still on his feet, clearly not sure what to do with himself.

"Huh?" McKinley asked, pulling back Grandma Bev's blanket. It was speckled with oatmeal, too, and impossible to clean with the thin paper towels from the holder.

"Do you think my mom will be able to drink the smoothie when Aunt Connie comes back?" Billy clarified. "So she doesn't need a feeding tube."

There was a fresh blanket in the closet beside the bed. McKinley shook it out. "There are no smoothies," she said. Gently, she tugged the dirty blanket off Grandma Bev's legs and replaced it with the new one. "At least, I didn't see any. I just made that up to get Aunt Connie out of here. Grab that end, will you?"

Billy tugged down his side of the blanket. "But why—?"

"Your mom'll eat the oatmeal fine," McKinley explained. "Just not the way Aunt Connie was doing it. Anyone would choke if they got force-fed like that." She went to smooth out the last of the blanket wrinkles, and to her surprise Grandma Bev's good hand found hers and gave it a little squeeze.

And she couldn't be totally sure, but McKinley thought she saw a *thank you* in Grandma Bev's eyes.

McKinley silently sent back a *you're welcome, love you*.

She turned back to the bowl of oatmeal Aunt Connie had slammed down on the end table and gave it a stir. "This is way too thick," she said. "Hand me that milk over there?" She gestured to the tray she'd brought in, and Billy stared at it for a while, like he couldn't tell milk from OJ. But finally he picked the right one. "Watch, okay?" she told him. She peeled the Saran Wrap off the milk and poured a tiny bit into the bowl. She stirred, then poured some more. "You're gonna have to be doing this soon, so you gotta see how to get the right consistency."

Billy walked over, gawking at McKinley's stirring like she was performing brain surgery. "How do you know all this?"

"My grandma had a stroke," she replied. "Usually she can do everything just fine, but she has bad days sometimes and needs help." McKinley pulled the spoon up and let the oatmeal stream off it—thicker than syrup but thinner than brownie batter. "That's probably good." Then she scooped a tiny amount—not even half a spoonful—and lifted it slowly to Grandma Bev's mouth. "This would be better warm," she told Bev, "sorry. But it's what we have right now. You ready?" Bev blinked. "Okay, you got this." And when Grandma Bev opened her mouth, McKinley tipped the oatmeal in. "That all right?" Grandma Bev nodded, just a fraction. "If you have trouble swallowing, I can massage your throat a little." She turned to Billy. "I'll show you that, too."

Bite by bite, swallow by swallow, Grandma Bev got half the bowl of oatmeal down. When she seemed to be perking up a bit, McKinley handed the bowl to Billy so he could practice. But he just stirred it.

"You can totally do this," McKinley assured him. "Just start with a tiny amount and—"

"I don't really think I need to learn this," Billy told her, holding out the bowl for McKinley to take back. "Aunt Connie said the doctor thinks my mom will be back to normal soon."

McKinley did not take the oatmeal. "She won't," she said softly.

Billy narrowed his eyes at her. "You think you're smarter than the doctor now?" he snapped, and McKinley did her best to remember that it wasn't really her he was mad at. "Maybe *your* grandma stayed sick, but my mom's strong. She'll be fine, you'll see. You have no idea what's gonna happen."

When he seemed good and ranted out, McKinley finally allowed herself to talk. "You're right," she told him. Billy was sinking back into his chair. McKinley took the bowl from him and stirred up the oatmeal even though it didn't need stirring. "I don't know the future." Which, maybe now, was true. How much had the future changed just from her being here? What would she find when she went back? "I just think . . ." McKinley glanced at Grandma Bev, who looked tired but surprisingly calm. "I think maybe you need to learn this stuff, just in case. I mean, you really want Aunt Connie to be in charge of everything?"

Billy let out a tiny snort. But he still wouldn't take the oatmeal when McKinley offered it again.

"Maybe I was wrong before," she said. "About trying to change everything. Maybe some things just happen, and there's nothing you can do about them." Even if McKinley had gotten to the house before the stroke, what could she have done? Yelled at that blood clot in her grandmother's brain to just quit it already? As terrible as Grandma Bev's stroke was, it wasn't a thing that McKinley—or anyone else—could've ever changed. "But maybe . . ." She glanced up at Billy again. His face was blotchy with tears. "Maybe when things happen that we can't change"—McKinley sat up a little straighter as the thought took hold—"maybe that's when *we* have to change with them."

For a long time, Billy only stared at his hands, saying nothing at all.

McKinley waited.

"What if I don't want anything to change?" he said at last.

Still, McKinley said nothing. Instead, she held out the bowl again.

This time, Billy took it.

He scraped a tiny amount of oatmeal onto the spoon and, arm shaking, brought it toward his mother's mouth.

"The trick is," McKinley told him softly, "figuring out what she needs without her being able to say it. You have to be able to tell if the food is too wet for her, or too dry. Either way, she could have trouble swallowing and choke. And it's best to do little meals spread throughout the day, instead of three big ones. You might need to write out a schedule or something."

"I hate schedules," Billy said.

And McKinley couldn't help it. She laughed.

Spoonful by tiny spoonful, Billy seemed to get the hang of things. McKinley felt like she could begin to see how the punk kid she met a week ago might, over time, turn into the rigid, schedule-obsessed father she was so familiar with. And yeah, that second guy could be hard to live with, but at least now it made some sort of sense to McKinley how he'd gotten there.

Maybe, McKinley thought, she never was meant to stop Billy from turning into her dad at all. Maybe she'd been sent back—right here, in this moment—to help him get there.

It was a weird thought.

Billy was almost done with the bowl of oatmeal, and doing a pretty good job, too, when there was a knock on the open door. They turned to see who was there.

"Good morning, Beverly," said the male doctor in the doorway. "You're looking much perkier than the last time I saw you." Grandma Bev offered the doctor her lopsided smile. She was still getting the hang of things, too. "I'm Dr. Kinney," he told McKinley and Billy. "I came in to give you all a lesson on feeding our star patient here"—he gestured to the oatmeal bowl in Billy's hands—"but I see someone else must've beaten me to it. You're quite the pro, young man." Billy's cheeks turned red. "Beverly, I can tell you're going to be in fine hands when you go home. You're lucky to have such capable children."

As Dr. Kinney took Grandma Bev's vitals, he made comfortable chitchat with Billy and McKinley—everything from the end of the school year to the Phillies' prospects to the weather. And somehow that morphed into: "Your mom won't be going home for a few days, I suspect. But she's definitely stable enough that you kids can make it to the Time Hop today, if you want. I hear it's going to be a good one."

McKinley's body shot up in her chair. "The Time Hop is today?" she said. Somehow, in the midst of everything, she'd lost track of time.

"Sure is," Dr. Kinney replied. "My wife and I have been working on our cos—"

But McKinley was already on her feet. "I have to go," she said. Because if this was the day she was going back, she had work to do—and quick. "I'm sorry," she told Billy. "I . . ." There weren't words to explain any of it. She turned to Grandma Bev. "I might not see you guys for a while," she told them. "A long time, I think. But I promise I'll see you again." And when Grandma Bev gave McKinley her familiar half smile, McKinley couldn't help herself. "I love you," she whispered, leaning in close to kiss her grandmother on the forehead. And if Grandma Bev thought that was weird, she didn't let on. She just squeezed McKinley's hand in hers.

"You're really leaving right now?" Billy asked. "For good?" He sounded upset.

"You'll be okay," she told him. McKinley hated that this was the moment she had to leave, but she didn't have much of a choice. "I promise. It will all turn out okay." And she gave him a big hug. Billy didn't even seem to mind.

As McKinley raced through the streets of Gap Bend, she did her best to push away any worries about Billy and Grandma Bev. There was a hard road ahead of them, but McKinley already knew they'd come out of it stronger than ever.

But as for Jackie—there was something McKinley needed to tell her, and it couldn't wait a single second.

McKinley picked up her pace, running faster than she'd ever run before.

30

Run to You

The whole way to the school, McKinley kept pinching herself, making sure she was still there. Which didn't make a whole lot of sense, obviously, because even if she had gone back to 2018, she'd still be there—that "there" would just be a whole lot different than "there" was here.

That was more than she could say for sure about Meg, though. When McKinley went back, Meg might not be here or there or anywhere.

McKinley needed to talk to Jackie before it was too late.

As soon as she stepped through the front door of Gap Bend Public School, McKinley breathed a sigh of relief. There was a group of volunteers in the entryway putting the finishing touches on their *Wizard of Oz* yellow brick road. A swinging jazz number echoed through the hall speakers. So McKinley had not been Time Hopped just yet.

"You're early," one of the volunteers told her. He was holding a pair of witchy legs in striped stockings that McKinley figured were meant to go underneath the tornadoed house along the wall. "The Time Hop doesn't start for two hours."

McKinley opened her mouth to explain that she wasn't there for the Time Hop (well, not exactly), but she was cut off by a voice from down the hall.

"Mickey's with me!" called Ms. Friedman, waving McKinley over.

McKinley hustled to join her.

"The rest of the committee is in the gym already," Ms. Friedman said. "Can you grab the costumes from the library for me and bring them down? It's the rack in the media closet. I'll meet you there after I fix the microphone situation. Have you seen Billy, by the way?"

McKinley tried to answer that, but Ms. Friedman was so frazzled that she scuttled right past the answer.

"You can roll the whole rack out the library's back door, okay? It should be open."

"Actually, I'm just here to—"

It was too late. Ms. Friedman was already halfway to the A/V room. "Thanks a million!" she told McKinley.

McKinley turned for the gym to find Jackie. But no sooner had she started down the humanities hall than she heard another voice—one she'd very much been hoping to avoid.

"If Ms. Friedman told you that you could borrow the books, then I'm certain they're there." It was Mr. Jones, growly as ever. McKinley's heart wrenched to a stop. She didn't have time to waste explaining why she shouldn't be hiding away in some dark corner. She had to get to Jackie before she was whisked away to her own millennium.

Fortunately, Mr. Jones had his head half-stuck in the door of his classroom as he yelled, so he didn't notice McKinley as she slid past him. *"Search the shelves, Miss Yorks! I can't be bothered with your nonsense."*

McKinley froze. *Miss Yorks?* As in Jackie Yorks?

Quickly, McKinley ducked behind a pillar, holding her breath as Mr. Jones spun on his heel and stomped past her. Then, when he was well out of sight, she darted into the classroom.

The light was off. McKinley didn't see Jackie anywhere.

"Jackie?" McKinley stepped farther into the room. "Are you here?"

Suddenly, McKinley heard a soft *click!* behind her. She whipped around to find the door shut tight—and, through the door's tiny window, Mr. Jones's pale face.

"You just stay in there," he told her through the glass. He looked sweaty, like this awful trick had taken every last nerve he had. "I'm not going to risk you altering anything else until you're back where you belong."

McKinley grabbed at the door handle. Locked. This was *not* happening.

"Let me out of here!" she shouted, banging on the glass.

"Sorry," Mr. Jones said. And he really did look sorry, but that didn't come close to making up for it. "This is the best thing for the universe. Trust me." McKinley could only watch helplessly as he peeled a 1939 advertisement for Brylcreem off the opposite wall and pasted it carefully over his classroom window.

Bang bang bang!

She couldn't see out of the room at all now—and worse, no one could see her.

"I'm going to go turn up the music in the hallway now," Mr. Jones called over McKinley's banging. "So it'll be no use making all that racket. No one's going to hear you."

McKinley offered the glass one last useless slap.

To her surprise, Mr. Jones peeled up the bottom corner of the advertisement to peer through the window. McKinley's breath caught in her throat. Maybe he was feeling some small bit of pity. Maybe he was going to let her out after all.

But all he said was, "If you get hungry, there's a Kudos bar in my desk drawer." And he pulled the ad down again.

There was, indeed, something called a "Kudos" bar in Mr. Jones's desk drawer. There was not, however, anything McKinley could use to pick the door lock.

In one of the kid desks, McKinley found a paper clip—but after ten minutes of trying, she had to admit that picking a lock wasn't nearly as easy as it looked on TV.

Next she tried the phone on the wall, but when she called the office, whoever picked up only shouted, "*What? Who is this? You're where? This dang music is so loud! Just come here if you need something, all right?*"

McKinley hung up.

The windows along the far wall of the classroom were swollen shut. They would jiggle, like they *wanted* to open—but as hard as she tugged, McKinley couldn't get them to budge. Not any of them.

So McKinley tried the fire extinguisher. That ought to be heavy enough to smash through a window, she figured. Only, when she chucked it at the glass, it actually *bounced back*.

McKinley shrieked and ducked just in time, pressing herself flat against the ugly brown linoleum.

McKinley sighed and pressed her cheek to the dirty floor. She couldn't believe she'd almost died from being smacked in the head by a boomerang fire extinguisher. Maybe she should just give up. Maybe the smartest thing was to stay right here, curled up on the floor, and enjoy the nice breeze drifting over her, until she finally . . .

McKinley sat up.

Breeze?

There was a single narrow window in the alcove behind Mr. Jones's desk that McKinley had overlooked before. And it appeared that Mr. Jones was about as terrible at trapping kids inside classrooms as McKinley was at escaping from them. Because that window was propped open, just a crack. It took some effort to wrench it up farther, but at last McKinley managed to get herself about ten inches of freedom.

It wasn't a lot, but it was enough.

31

I Keep Coming Back

O*of!*" McKinley grunted as she tumbled out of the window into the prickly bushes below. She brushed herself off, discovering that there was now a full-blown hole in the knee of Jackie's black tights. Just one more thing for Jackie to be angry about.

The back entrance to the gym wasn't far way. McKinley hunched low as she ran in case Mr. Jones happened to look outside. But when she got there, the heavy steel door was locked tight. Shoot.

She tugged and tugged at the door handle uselessly for a few seconds, then changed course and pressed her face to the window nearby, squinting past the grime.

The gym had been transformed into a 1939 wonderland. There was a working newspaper press in one corner and an old-timey cinema in another, with red-velvet seats and a huge movie screen with plush curtains. People were hustling this way and that, finishing up different projects. The Student Volunteer Committee was there, too. Chanel was fixing her hair. Darla and Ron appeared to be going over lines. And there was Jackie— watching Alyse turn cartwheels, like it was a perfectly normal Saturday morning. Like she *didn't* know that the person who'd been spending the whole last week on her bedroom floor was about to up and vanish into thin air.

McKinley banged hard on the window, until her fist ached.

With a start, a face appeared on the other side of the glass.

"Ron!" McKinley gasped. "Let me in, will you?"

"Mickey?" He looked confused. "We were wondering where you were! Have you seen Billy? I called his house, and no one answered."

McKinley swallowed. "His mom . . ." she told Ron. "She got sick. But he's going to be okay." Ron's eyebrows knit together with concern. "Can you open the door, please? I really need to talk to Jackie."

Ron left the window briefly but came right back. "It's locked!" he told her. "You'll have to go around to the front."

But McKinley knew she couldn't risk it. What if she ran into Mr. Jones again?

"Can you tell Jackie to come over here really quick?" she asked. "It's important."

Ron gave her an *Aye-aye!* salute, then skittered off.

McKinley watched as he spoke to Jackie. And she kept watching, too, as Jackie looked up toward McKinley at the window. Even through the distance and the grime, McKinley could see the sneer on Jackie's face as she shook her head—a hard no.

By the time Ron made it back to the window, McKinley's heart had sunk lower than her toes.

"She's, uh, busy," he told her. "Can't you just use the other door?"

"I don't have time." McKinley felt like she might burst with all she needed to say. "Listen, Ron, this is important, okay?" He nodded. "You have to tell Jackie I'm sorry. Will you tell her for me?" He nodded again. "And tell her she was right. It's not my job to change her." Even if McKinley wanted—needed—Meg in her life, in the world, it wasn't hers to make happen. That's what she'd finally realized, watching her dad at the hospital. The world wasn't hers alone to change—everyone had to make their own choices. So even if it meant that McKinley's life would end up being so awful that just thinking about it made her want to sink into a hole and disappear forever, McKinley knew she had to stop twisting everyone else's life up just to make hers better. And it was important, too, that Jackie knew she knew it.

"And can you tell her one more thing?" she asked Ron. "This is the most important one. Tell her I said 'Olive 1—'"

"*Not again!*"

McKinley's head shot to the left. There was Mr. Jones, hustling toward her faster than any sixth-grade history teacher in khaki pants had a right to go.

McKinley bolted.

She raced around one corner of the school, then another, till she spotted an open door. The library. She darted inside, her chest heaving. The librarian, Mr. Deisler, was behind the circulation desk, but he hadn't noticed her coming in. McKinley would have to keep it that way, or he might tell Mr. Jones where she'd gone.

Thinking quickly, McKinley darted to the door marked MEDIA CLOSET and slipped inside. When she shut the door behind her, she was sunk into darkness. She held her breath, squished up against the rack of costumes—silky, scratchy, soft—and waited for the sound of Mr. Jones's angry stomping to pass her by.

She waited.

And waited.

Nothing.

After several minutes, McKinley pressed her ear to the door to listen. Not a step, not a whisper. Was it possible Mr. Jones had raced past the library door without turning inside? But even if McKinley were lucky enough for that to be true, she'd never make it back to the gym without him spotting her.

Unless . . . he thought he was looking for someone else?

Her heart beating hard, McKinley flipped on the light switch. She held her breath, listening again. Still nothing. She turned to the rack of costumes. Maybe, just maybe, there was something here that would disguise her enough so she could slip through the hallway unnoticed. A giant coat, maybe. Or a big hat. She and Billy had picked out some good '30s-looking hats at the thrift store.

But as she flicked through the outfits, she didn't see a single thing that would help. A long-sleeve bodysuit. A neon track jacket. A pair of gaudy parachute pants.

Wait a minute.

McKinley whipped through the hangers again. Why were there oversize flannels and high-waisted jeans? It should've been all flowery dresses and men's suits with fat collars.

Slowly, McKinley turned. Slowly, she opened the closet door. And slower than slow, she stepped back out into the library and looked around.

Mr. Deisler, the librarian, was no longer there. Neither was the wooden card catalog. Or the boxy gray computers. Gone, too, were the beat-up filing cabinets and the poster of Denzel Washington reading *Green Eggs and Ham*. Instead, the READ posters now featured Misty Copeland and Daveed Diggs—people who weren't exactly poster worthy in 1993. And there was the rolling tablet-charging station. And the flat-screen TV hanging high on the far wall. Everything was just as McKinley had always known it.

She was back. Or rather, *forward*. McKinley had returned to 2018, where she'd always belonged.

She should've felt relieved.

But instead, McKinley just felt tired.

She made her way over to a wooden library chair and sank down into it, resting her head on the hard round table. And she sat there, not even thinking, really, just breathing, refusing to lift her head. Because when she did, McKinley knew that she'd have to begin to suss out what else was different about the world now. And she didn't think she was ready for that yet.

Maybe not ever.

And so McKinley didn't look up when she heard the library door creak open. And she didn't look up, still, when she heard the footsteps making their way to her table. Or when she felt the warm hand on her shoulder.

"McKinley?"

"Go away," McKinley muttered into her arms.

"Oh, McKinley, I'm so glad you're back. I've been looking everywhere for you!"

Grown-up Jackie had that same lilt to her voice as the twelve-year-old version, but she sounded different, too. Deeper, slightly. More concerned, definitely.

"Are you okay, honey?"

McKinley breathed in the smell of her own arm. "I don't know," she admitted. Her stomach hurt.

"McKinley, you gotta look at me, okay?" Jackie said. "Otherwise I'm gonna think you grew an extra nose on the trip back or something."

Slowly, McKinley lifted her head.

"Oh, thank God," Jackie said. And McKinley let herself be squeezed into a hug. It felt nice being hugged by grown-up Jackie again. But McKinley knew that nice feeling couldn't last forever.

She swallowed hard, forcing herself to pull out of that safe, warm hug. She looked at Jackie, taking in the fine wrinkles in the corners of her eyes. The darkened spots that had speckled her skin over the past twenty-five years.

And she asked.

"Is Meg here?"

McKinley clenched her stomach.

Waited.

Jackie reached out and wiped a tear from underneath McKinley's right eye.

"No," she told her.

32

It's Alright

Here's what it feels like when all the air is sucked out of your body: You can't breathe, obviously. But it's more than that. Your lungs collapse so tight that they feel like they'll never be able to expand and let in any air ever again. It's like your lungs are all, *Well, air was nice when we had it, but I guess it's gone for good now.* Meanwhile, your brain is going, *Um, lungs? Helloooooo? Where's the air at?* And while your brain is busy battling it out with your lungs, your eyesight starts to dim, then blacken, and soon you're in full-blown panic mode.

"McKinley! McKinley! Breathe! You have to breathe!"

Somehow, Jackie managed to shake McKinley hard enough that her lungs snapped back into action. Her brain got the precious air it needed, and her eyes focused on the world once more. Somehow, McKinley saw now, she was a puddle on the floor. She wasn't quite sure how it had happened, but there she was, limp and soggy.

"It's okay, honey. It's okay." Jackie was on the floor right next to her, rubbing her back in smooth circles. "I didn't mean— Meg's alive, honey. She's just not here."

McKinley dared to look up. She wiped at her nose.

"Her dad took her to the FACTS competition," Jackie went

on. She was still wearing her ugly white nylon tracksuit from the Time Hop. "They left a little while ago. You've been gone since morning."

McKinley sniffled. "I didn't wipe her out of existence?" she asked.

Jackie let out a gentle laugh. "No, she exists, all right. I remember the moment she came into the world quite well." She must've been able to tell that McKinley was still worried, though, because she dug her phone out of her pocket. "See?" Jackie handed over her phone, letting McKinley flick through the photos.

Sure enough, there was Meg, blowing out the candles at her last birthday party. Doing a handstand in her favorite shirt with the roller-skating llama on it. And there she was with McKinley, the two of them making goofy faces for the camera. McKinley took a deep, calming breath—*in, out, in out*—and her brain thanked her for the air.

"And Grandma Bev?" McKinley asked. "She's okay? She got her medicine this afternoon?"

Jackie leaned over and swiped to a photo from that very day—Grandma Bev playing *Street Fighter II* with Ron. "Never been better," she said.

"And my dad? And Ron? And . . . you?"

Jackie smiled. "Fine, fine, and extra fine," she said. "Well, I'm fine now that I know you're back. I told your dad I'd hang out with you until you cooled off, and for a hot second there, I thought you might never return and I'd have to tell your dad some wild story about you running off to babysit Beyoncé's twins." She took the phone back from McKinley. "How about we call him, let him know you're okay? You must be ready to get back home. You've had a long day. Er, week."

"Can you take me to see Meg first?" McKinley asked as Jackie found the number in her phone.

"You want to go to the competition?" Jackie said.

McKinley nodded slowly. "I have something I need to say to Meg. And it really can't wait." She glanced at the time on Jackie's phone. "You think we can make it there before it starts?"

Jackie thought about it. "I've been known to break the speed limit occasionally," she told McKinley, lifting the phone to her ear. Then she lowered it. "Don't tell your dad that part," she added.

And even though they were in a rush, McKinley thought it was worth the extra five seconds to give Jackie an enormous hug. "Thank you," she told her.

"Any time," Jackie replied.

Somehow, Jackie convinced McKinley's dad that he should let McKinley go to the competition—which, as far as McKinley was concerned, was even more astonishing than the existence of time travel.

As soon as they left the library, McKinley could hear the sound of music wafting out from the gym—"*Hey, Mr. DJ, keep playing that song!*" Clearly the Time Hop was still in full swing. McKinley, however, had had enough of the '90s for a while. And they were nearly to the main doors, with the enormous dinosaur statues in front, when McKinley spotted another thing she'd had enough of.

When Mr. Jones spotted McKinley across the hall, he shook his finger at her and shouted, "*Aha!*" Like he'd caught her red-handed at something, when the only thing she was doing was walking.

"Mr. Jones," Jackie said, her voice tired. "Can we just quit it with this, already? McKinley's back now, and we have places to be."

He frowned. "You're not going anywhere until you tell me exactly wh—"

"No," McKinley said.

Mr. Jones stopped. He opened his mouth slowly, like he couldn't believe what he was hearing. "What did you say?" he asked her.

"I said, no," she repeated. What was he going to do, give her a D in history? "I don't need to tell you anything. Not now. Right now what I need to do is see my best friend."

"I don't think so." Mr. Jones shifted himself in front of the open double doors, like he thought he could tackle them if they tried to get by.

"Don't make me lock you in the closet again," Jackie told him.

McKinley couldn't help but snort at that. "Maybe we're even now," she told her teacher, "with locking each other up." And she pushed past him into the fresh night air. Maybe it was because he was so much older than when she'd last seen him or because she'd lived twenty-five years in one afternoon, but whatever the reason, McKinley didn't find him so threatening anymore. "Goodbye, Mr. Jones!" she told him as she bounded down the stairs.

He did not try to stop her.

But as McKinley and Jackie raced to the car, he did call after her, *"But what did you change?"* His voice split through the crisp June evening. *"What did you change?"*

33

Changes

M cKinley kept her eyes peeled as they drove, but she couldn't find a single thing that wasn't exactly how she remembered it. No stoplights out of place. No new shopping centers. Not even an unfamiliar song on the radio. She flipped through Jackie's phone, searching for anything that seemed off. But everything was just the same. Same photos. Same apps. She scrolled through Jackie's news feed. Same, same, same.

But hadn't she stepped on plenty of butterflies while she was gone? Surely *something* must be different now because of her?

McKinley was concentrating so hard on scouring Meg's Instagram account for signs of change that when Jackie began to speak, she jumped in her seat.

"I'm sorry I never told you, by the way," Jackie said. "I went back and forth about it, but ultimately I decided it was best not to say anything."

McKinley was scrutinizing a photo of Meg holding her aunt's pet ferret. "Say anything about what?" she asked, only half listening.

Jackie paused a moment, switching lanes. "About you going back in time," she said.

McKinley dropped the phone. "You *knew?*" she asked.

Jackie nodded. "I've known you were going to time travel since I was twelve years old. I had no idea how it was going to end, though. *That* was a real nail-biter, waiting for you to get back." She switched lanes again. "You know what? I'm not even going to bother with 476 this time of night. Surface roads'll be way faster."

McKinley squinted at the side of Jackie's head. "So this whole time," she said, trying to wrap her mind around it, "when you were, like, driving me and Meg to tap lessons or playing Crazy Eights with us or during that water balloon war we had last summer, you were thinking, 'That girl's about to time travel'?"

Jackie checked her mirrors. "Pretty much," she said.

McKinley slapped her knees. She was still wearing Jackie's black tights with the hole in them. "You could've at least *warned* me!" she said.

Jackie wrinkled her nose like she wasn't totally sure about her decision either. "I almost did like a thousand times," she admitted. "But in the end, I figured it was best if you didn't know what was going to happen, if you just experienced it—the way you were experiencing it when I first met you."

"Does my dad know?" McKinley wondered.

"Are you kidding?" Jackie replied. "*I* wasn't gonna be the one to tell him. That guy gets nervous if you eat too many nachos at a sleepover." McKinley had to laugh at that. "Nope, I never told a soul. I did make sure you always knew my home was a safe space, though."

If you ever need my help, you can come find me, anytime.

"Well, thanks," McKinley said. She snatched the phone off the ground and set it in the cup holder between them. "It was nice to have one friend, at least, while I was . . ."

Wait a minute.

"Aren't you mad at me?" she asked Jackie. "The last time we talked, we—"

"The last time we talked," Jackie cut in, "was twenty-five years ago. I've had some time to think on things. And I like to think I've grown up a little."

"I'm still sorry," McKinley said. "For what I said back there. Back then," she corrected. "I shouldn't have said those things, about your writing and not having friends . . ." McKinley's stomach felt sour just remembering all of it.

"I'm sorry, too," Jackie told her. "I was kind of a hothead when I was a kid."

McKinley snorted.

"Anyway," Jackie went on, "you were right about lots of it. Me and Ron, for starters. Although, believe me, I tried my hardest *not* to fall in love with him."

"So what happened?" McKinley asked.

"Time, mainly," Jackie told her. "I got older. He got older. Sophomore year of high school, we sat next to each other in English and we bonded over our mutual hatred of *The Scarlet Letter*. And when my date to the winter formal came down with mono, I asked Ronny to go with me as a friend, and he said yes. That's when I realized that goofballs were a lot of fun to hang out with. We tangoed all over the dance floor during the slow dances. Ron even stuffed my corsage between his teeth like a rose." McKinley grinned. That sounded like the Ron and Jackie she knew. "But I still made it very clear to him that I wasn't interested in being anything but friends." She glanced sideways at McKinley. "See, *someone* had told me I was going to marry Little Ronny Rothstein one day, and I wanted to prove to myself that I didn't have to do something just because a time traveler told me I should."

"But . . . ?" McKinley prompted.

"It turned out that marrying Little Ronny Rothstein *was* the thing I wanted," Jackie told her. "It took me long enough, but I finally figured out that I *did* have a choice in how my life turned out—I had just been making bad choices. So I got over myself and asked him out. For our first official date, we went to the Galaxy Arcade and played *Street Fighter II*." Her cheeks flushed, happy with the memory. "It was pretty sweet."

McKinley scratched an itch at the back of her neck, thinking. "So . . . I didn't do anything, then?" she wondered. "I mean, whether I'd met you in the past or not, you would've ended up with Ron either way. Meg would've been born no matter what."

Jackie drummed her fingers on the steering wheel. "Maybe," she said. "And maybe not. I've spent a *lot* of time chewing it all over, and of course, I can't know for sure, but here's my theory." She checked her mirrors and switched lanes again. "I don't think time travel works the way we thought it did—where changing something in your past changes what will happen in the future."

"So how does it work, then?"

"Well, what if time isn't a straight line?" Jackie answered. "What if it's more like a circle?"

Which didn't exactly clear things up.

"Huh?" McKinley wondered.

"If time is a circle," Jackie went on, "then the things that happen in our past aren't behind us the way we usually think of them. They're behind us and ahead of us *at the same time*."

"My head hurts," McKinley replied.

Jackie laughed. "Fair enough. But okay, think of it this way. What if the reason you went back in time was *not* because of some glitch in the universe or even because some all-knowing magic whoever-whatever wanted you to do something important? What if the reason you went back in time was because *you already had*?"

McKinley's eyebrows shot up. "I'm still kind of stuck on 'Huh?'"

"The way I see it," Jackie explained, "the reason your present reality—this, right here—is the way it is, and the reason nothing seems different now that you're back, is because *you* made it that way. The things you did way back in 1993 created this reality—the one where I married Ron and your dad is an awesome caretaker and you're a cool, thoughtful kid who loves to sew and has a fabulous best friend. It's all because of things that *you* did, decisions *you* made, before you were even born. Only, you had no idea that it was all due to you—because you hadn't done any of it yet. Well, you had, and you hadn't. Because time is a circle. See?"

McKinley took a deep, calm breath. *In, out. In, out.* "Huh," she said. But it wasn't a question this time. "So . . ." McKinley focused on the world outside the window, looking just the same as it had always been. "I changed everything, but also nothing? Because all the stuff I changed—I'd already changed it. I mean, if what you're saying is true." Jackie stayed quiet, letting McKinley work through the creaky thoughts. "And if I only did all those things just because I'd done them before"—she scratched at her neck again—"was I really even deciding anything?"

Jackie nodded. "I have some aspirin in my purse if your headache gets too bad," she said.

As they crossed the bridge into the city, past Boathouse Row, it began to rain, slowly at first, then harder. McKinley found herself wondering about all those raindrops, falling to the ground just to get washed out to sea and sucked back up into the clouds again. A never-ending circle. It was beautiful but kind of sad, too. Like the raindrops didn't have any choice in the matter.

They reached the convention center, and Jackie pulled into a miraculously open parking spot. She shifted into park, then turned off the ignition.

"Look," Jackie told McKinley. "I can only imagine how weird this has been for you. And I don't know how you're going to manage things going forward. But I will tell you what I've learned from you, both way back in middle school and from getting to know you as you've grown up." She unclicked her seat belt and turned to better face McKinley. "You, McKinley O'Dair, are one special person. You are kind and creative and smart and silly. And when you make mistakes, you try your hardest to fix them."

McKinley watched a slurry of raindrops drizzling their way down her side window. "I guess," she said softly. She moved to open her door.

But Jackie wasn't done.

"*And*," she went on, "having you as a friend when I was in sixth grade made my life a million times better."

McKinley turned to look at her. "It did?" she asked.

"Absolutely," Jackie told her. And then, as though she'd read McKinley's mind: "But I don't think that's probably the *reason* you went back—if there was a reason. And it wasn't to change your dad either. If you *were* meant to change somebody, I think it was someone much more important."

McKinley wrinkled her nose. "Mr. Jones?" she guessed.

Jackie laughed hard. "Definitely not."

"Then who?"

Jackie offered McKinley a knowing smile. "I have no doubt you'll figure it out," she told her. "When you're ready." And with that, she grabbed her phone from the cup holder. She checked the time. "Shoot. They're starting." She flung open her door.

But McKinley didn't move.

"You coming?" Jackie asked, poking her head back in the car. Her hair was already half-soaked.

"One sec," McKinley told her.

There was a single raindrop, McKinley noticed, that was making a curious zigzag path down the glass of her window. A slight hitch to the left of the other drops, an unmistakable path all its own.

McKinley dug into her pocket—Jackie's pocket, really, of the shorts she'd borrowed all those years ago. And she found the note, the heart-shaped one she'd meant to slip into Ron's backpack so he'd think Jackie loved him.

McKinley handed it to Jackie.

"This is for you," she told her. "I should've given it to you a while ago."

Carefully, Jackie unfolded the heart. And she read the words.

I'm sorry about how I acted. I actually think you're pretty great, and I promise to do a better job of showing it.

Jackie pressed the note to her chest, keeping it safe from the rain.

"I think you're pretty great, too, kid," she told McKinley.

And McKinley smiled at that. Because maybe the raindrop would get sucked right back into the clouds one day—but that didn't mean it couldn't make waves before then.

McKinley opened her door.

She had some waves to make, too.

34

Back Together Again

D id we miss her?" McKinley whispered as she and Jackie slipped into the seats Ron had saved up front. Round one of the FACTS competition was already well underway, and McKinley couldn't believe she'd lost her one opportunity to talk to Meg beforehand.

Ron shook his head. "There are still two people before her turn," he whispered back.

It wasn't long before the judge called Meg up to the mic. McKinley clapped so hard she felt like her hands might fall off. Jackie whooped. But up on the stage, Meg wasn't standing. Instead, she stayed firmly rooted to her chair. Her knee was bouncing a mile a minute.

"Margaret Rothstein?" the judge repeated. "It's your turn."

McKinley knew Meg always got nervous before she answered a question, but she'd never seen her like *this*. No matter how petrified Meg was, she always took a deep breath, locked eyes with McKinley, and stood up.

That was the difference, McKinley realized. For the first time ever, McKinley wasn't up on the stage with her.

But maybe McKinley could still find a way to help.

Snatching the pen that Ron had been twirling nervously,

McKinley pressed her program open flat. Then, in the biggest, thickest letters she could manage, she scribbled out a note for her best friend.

"Meg!" McKinley hollered into the silence.

On the stage, Meg's head jerked up. Her gaze landed on McKinley and on the words she'd written.

OLIVE LOAF!

Meg grinned the tiniest of grins.

She took a deep breath.

And she stepped up to the mic.

"You were *amazing*!" McKinley squealed, tackling Meg with a running hug as soon as she spotted her in the lobby after the competition. "I can't believe you're going to DC! That last question about dandelions was a doozy. You're a shoo-in for national champ."

Meg blushed. "Thanks," she said. "And, um"—she turned her gaze to her shoes—"thanks for coming. I wasn't sure you would."

McKinley knew it was time to say the thing she'd waited much too long to say. "I'm really sorry," she told Meg. "About lying, about everything." She cleared her throat. It would've been so easy to stop there, but she made herself press on. "I don't want to do FACTS next year," she admitted, and Meg frowned. "It's not really my thing anymore. But I should've just told you that. And just because I don't want to do it anymore doesn't mean you can't. I mean, you know that already"—she rubbed her left arm with her right hand—"but I guess I needed to figure it out. And I don't think you need to 'shake things up,' either. Unless you want to. Because you're great exactly how you are, and trying to force you to change into someone else wasn't very . . ." McKinley trailed off, not sure how to express how rotten and silly and dense she'd been.

Meg was nodding slowly. "I'm sorry, too," she told McKinley. Which McKinley definitely was not expecting. "Friends again?"

"Um, duh," McKinley said with a laugh. "Because you know why?"

And that time, they both said it, at the exact same time.

"Olive loaf!"

"Pretzel point!"

"Pretzel point!"

"PRETZEL POINT!"

McKinley finally won, but only because Meg suddenly stopped trying. She'd grabbed one edge of McKinley's oversize flannel shirt and was taking in McKinley's whole outfit—cutoff shorts, black tights with the rip in the knee, white tee, all of it.

"Did you change?" Meg asked her.

And at that, McKinley couldn't help but smile.

"Yeah," she told her friend. "I guess I did."

35

You Mean the World to Me

It was late by the time McKinley got home that night. When she opened the front door, her dad was sitting at the living room table scrolling through his phone with a scowl.

He looked up at her.

"You are *very* grounded," he told McKinley.

And McKinley nodded at that. "Okay," she said. And then: "I'm really sorry."

Her dad tilted his head, like he was sure McKinley must be up to something.

She stood in the doorway, thinking through her words carefully, her hands in her back pockets.

"I was talking to Meg," she said, "about how I messed up some stuff with her. Like, I think I was trying to . . . change her? Turn her into the kind of person I thought she *should* be? And obviously I shouldn't've been doing that." She looked up at her dad. At his slightly crooked nose, a souvenir from a truly awful day. "I guess I was trying to do that to you, too. I thought if you were different, it might make my life better." She took a deep, calm breath, inhaling a little extra bravery. "I think maybe you might've been doing the same thing to me."

Her father didn't say anything. He blinked at her, rubbing his crooked nose.

Slowly, as though trying not to spook a skittish puppy, McKinley crossed the room to the table. She pulled out the chair across from her dad. And she sat.

"I know schedules are important to you," she said. "And I think I actually get that now, more than I did." She pressed on. "But the thing is, there's stuff that's important to me, too."

Her dad finally did say something then.

"Mmm."

That's what he said.

But instead of throwing her hands up in the air, like she might've done before, McKinley stayed calm.

"Do you think we could ever compromise sometimes?" she asked.

And to McKinley's surprise, her father didn't *mmm* again.

Instead, he said, "That sounds fair." Then he paused. "After you're done being grounded. I'm not compromising on that."

McKinley nodded. "Deal."

"You know," her dad went on, "I didn't leave work this morning so I could embarrass you or make you miserable. When you didn't answer your phone, I was really worried."

McKinley bit the insides of her cheeks. It hadn't even occurred to her that might be the reason he'd done what he had. "I'm sorry," she said again.

"You shouldn't have behaved that way, McKinley," her dad replied. "That was irresponsible and immature. But . . ."

McKinley held her breath. There was a "but"?

"I shouldn't have behaved the way I did either," he went on. "I'm not proud of how I handled things today, and I owe you an apology for that." McKinley nearly pinched herself to make sure she hadn't entered into an alternate reality or something—but she was afraid of moving even an inch, not wanting to distract her dad. "I'm sorry, McKinley," he said. "You're very important to me." And for the first time all day, her dad smiled, a tiny little smile. "I hope you know that."

McKinley had missed that smile.

"You're important to me, too, Dad," she told him. And when he held out his arms, she scooched back her chair and headed over for a hug.

"I love you," he said into her hair.

"Love you back," she whispered.

That's when McKinley noticed her grandmother wheeling in from the hallway. "Grandma Bev!" she cried, racing over. "I thought you'd be asleep already."

Grandma Bev reached for McKinley's right hand with her left one, and she gave it a warm squeeze. She had so much more light in her eyes than when McKinley had last seen her at the hospital. "Guh—good to huh—have yuh—you buh—buh—back," she said. And then she added, with her familiar half smile, "Muh—Muh—Mickey."

McKinley sucked in her breath. Did her grandmother know somehow? Or had she just misspoken?

"You know, McKinley," her dad said, coming over to join them, "you missed some real drama at the Time Hop today. There was this kid there—I'd never seen him before—going on and on about the strangest stuff."

"Oh, yeah?" McKinley asked.

"Yeah," her dad said. "Something about how we should all be bracing ourselves for a global pandemic?"

And McKinley wasn't totally positive, but she could've sworn that Grandma Bev winked at her.

She turned her attention to her father. "Tell me *everything*," she said.

OUTRO

Now & Forever

One week later, McKinley gently rolled Grandma Bev up onto the curb in front of the Gap Bend Cineplex, her father at her side. When he read the title on the marquee out front—JURASSIC PARK: TWENTY-FIFTH ANNIVERSARY SCREENING!—McKinley's dad glanced down at Grandma Bev and rubbed hard at his crooked nose.

"You sure you're up for this, Dad?" McKinley asked. She could tell by the look on his face that he was probably remembering some hard things. (She wondered if he remembered a girl named Mickey who'd helped him out that day, too.)

For a long moment, McKinley was certain her dad was going to say no, he wasn't up for it, and they should go back home. Which would've been disappointing, of course. But McKinley would've understood.

Instead, he pulled his hand away from his face and turned to McKinley. "Let's do this," he said.

Miguel waved as they stepped up to the ticket booth. They could've bought their tickets from the touch screen machines inside, but McKinley had discovered that she liked doing some things the old-fashioned way.

"Nice to see you back at the theater, Mr. O'Dair," Miguel said as he handed McKinley's dad the tickets. "It's been a while." Then he leaned close to the plexiglass and lowered his voice. "Just promise me you won't do anything, uh, *explosive*, like last time?"

The back of McKinley's dad's neck went bright red. "Oh. Gosh. I'm so sorry about that."

Miguel only laughed. "It's okay," he reassured McKinley's dad. "You've served your time."

"What was that about?" McKinley asked. Like she didn't know exactly.

"Let's just say I've changed a lot since the nineties," her dad replied.

As it turned out, McKinley had changed a lot, too.

Well, she was trying.

Ever since she'd returned from her *Stupendous Time-Travel Adventure*, McKinley had been mostly grounded at home, with no screens and no sewing machine. Which, as it turned out, was the perfect opportunity to get to work crabbifying herself. Her journal was now filled with pages and pages of blessings she'd counted and ways she could attempt to right her past wrongs. She'd assessed her neighbors, too, and brainstormed some good ways to better her world. Starting on Monday, she was going to put her caretaking skills to good use and join Aunt Connie on her weekly trips to the local retirement center—which would also help McKinley shake up her routine. It was hard work, changing yourself instead of the people around you. But so far, it seemed to be worth it.

And even though he might never admit it, McKinley could tell that her dad was trying to change, too. He'd even conceded to one "wild card" night on the weekly dinner schedule, where McKinley and Grandma Bev could try out new recipes or even order a pizza. It might not seem like much to most people, but McKinley knew that, for her dad, it was a huge crabby step.

Meg and her parents were waiting for them just past the ticket taker. "You got him in the door!" Meg whispered to McKinley, offering her a thumbs-up. "Nice!"

McKinley's dad pulled his wallet out of his pocket. "Do you want any candy?" he asked. "I could maybe go for some plain M&M's."

"Oh, no, no, no," Jackie cut in. "William, I am about to blow your mind." She held out one of the two jumbo popcorn bags she was holding. Kernels spilled from the top of the overstuffed bag.

He squinched his mouth to one side. "I've had popcorn before," he said.

"Sure," Jackie agreed. They were so kind to each other now. You'd never know that they had once been mortal enemies. "But have you ever had *ranch-flavored* popcorn?"

McKinley's dad took the bag and sniffed it. "Oh, good God."

McKinley laughed. "They have these flavor shakers," she said, pointing to the assortment by the butter dispenser. "There's a bunch, but ranch is the best. Jackie has a special secret to make it taste amazing."

Jackie leaned in close to McKinley's dad and fake whispered, "The secret is using *tons* of it."

"I don't know . . ." McKinley's dad said warily.

"Okay, how about this?" McKinley compromised. "You try the ranch popcorn, and if you hate it, we'll get the M&M's? I'm sure Jackie wouldn't mind having extra."

"She would not," Jackie confirmed.

Her father thought about that. "Deal," he said, plucking a kernel out of the bag. He let it settle on his tongue. "Actually, that's . . ." He took another. "Surprisingly not awful."

"Told you," Jackie replied.

"I stand corrected."

As they settled into their seats—McKinley tucked happily between her dad and Meg, with Grandma Bev in the wheelchair spot beside them—McKinley allowed herself to sink into a feeling of deep happiness. Here she was, with all her very favorite people, exactly where she was meant to be. Exactly *when*. And to think that just one week ago, she'd been so absolutely miserable.

It just went to show you, McKinley thought as she stuffed her mouth full of ranch-flavored popcorn. Anyone could change, really, as long as they were allowed to do it their own way.

Sometimes, it just took a little time.